# Bronte

Thomas M. Barron

Garbage Wagon LLC
San Francisco, CA

**Bronte**

**Copyright © 2019 THOMAS M. BARRON**

*All rights reserved. No part of this book may be reproduced or transmitted in any form or by any means, electronic or mechanical, including photocopying, recording or by any information storage and retrieval system, without permission in writing from the author.*

**Cover art by David Powell**
**Creative Director Toby Petersen**
**Editor Jennifer Lewis**
**Polish Editor Maddy Hutchison**

**Published by**
**GARBAGE WAGON LLC**
San Francisco, CA

*This is a work of fiction. Names, characters, businesses, places, events and incidents are either the products of the author's imagination or used in a fictitious manner. Any resemblance to actual persons, living or dead, or actual events is purely coincidental.*

Library of Congress Control Number: 2018904195
ISBN (print): 978-0-9997033-1-1
ISBN (ebook): 978-0-9997033-2-8

Printed in the United States of America
1 3 5 7 9 10 8 6 4 2

*For our roommates that depart*
*but never leave us.*

# 1

*@unemployedlifecoach the girl i'm dating wants to take a vacation together. seems like a big step. should i go?*

*@AskEsquire If you have to ask, you're not ready. Take her camping overnight. For two nights. Then book the cruise.*

The last flight was the longest. Four in a row, from Panama to Australia. Endless layovers and overflowing aisles.

The Sydney airport Duty Free is a welcome reprieve, and the vodka aisle calls my name.

"Would you like to buy anothah at half price?" She holds up the bottle of Absolut.

"Yeah, and if they're that cheap, let's make it Grey Goose."

"Nice one! They're all boxed up special for Chrissy!" Chrissy =

Christmas, not vodka cobranded with my girlfriend from middle school.

"Perfect. I can't believe it's already December."

"Great time to take a holiday! Have a wondahful trip!"

She's that friendly.

I'm a little nervous to meet Suzanne, so I burn five with the free airport Wi-Fi.

Logging into my email gives me a bird's eye view of my hands on the keyboard. They've seen better days.

Burnt skin from where the bullet grazed my wrist. The scars on my hands from pulling PJ underwater, across razor-sharp barnacles, to safety. But it wasn't enough.

Over the past few weeks, my wounds have healed. My hands miraculously work. I can type, and I took my first legit swim a few days ago. But there are a lot of scars. Especially the big one on my heart.

PJ was my best friend. What an understatement. And I'm here. And hopefully I can help. Do something. Anything.

PJ's family will be addressed shortly. Very shortly. For now, I can escape for twenty seconds with work.

---

From: Rogers, Timothy

To: Georgeous

Subject: Transition

Attachment: Public Communications Guidelines.pdf

George—

We were looking forward to having you in New York next week, but I certainly understand your desire to attend PJ's services.

I can see from our Twitter feed that you were able to get up and running. If you could continue while you're away, it would help immensely. I've attached our guidelines, which can be summarized in one sentence: don't publish anything that will land us in court.

Let me know when you get settled, and we can discuss your proper return to the States.

Best,

TR

PS Please send Lydia the address for PJ's family. Esquire would like to send flowers or a donation, if more appropriate.

PPS Going forward, do start using your esquire.com email address. It will be much tamer than "Georgeous", even though I am a fan.

---

Tim (TR) is a rare bird. I used to think he was my nemesis at UCLA. As it turns out, he's just a good guy that knows how to play the game.

I try Yelp, using the Bronte 2024 zip code, and it works. The results for Swimming Pools all look like Photoshopped magazine covers.

The woman next to me barks into her phone. Thank god for high-end earphones. I slip on the Beats that I bought at the Singapore airport. Impulse buys occasionally restore sanity.

I finish and head to customs.

Quick recap: I ran away from my cheating girlfriend in LA to Bocas del Toro, Panama. It was great. A lot of swimming in warm water and serving drinks to tourists. After a year, I got sucked into a Mossad anti-terrorist plot and witnessed both my boss, Raúl, and best friend, PJ, get gunned down. I came to Sydney to go to PJ's funeral and to check in on his love child—Charlotte. I hope she's the only one. PJ had a lot of overnight guests. Although he was a philanderer, he was a family man. PJ would not have left his own offspring behind, knowingly.

This all sounds insane. Especially since I just flew over the crisp waters of Sydney Harbour.

•

I use my shoulder to open the baggage claim exit door.

Suzanne.

PJ's sister.

I see her. She's looking for me at the other exit. It gives me a chance to take her in, while she's still a stranger.

PJ's long ringlet hair was always more suited to a female, and she wears it well. They don't really have the same face. But the eyes. They're alert. And striking. And confident. And sad.

"Suzanne?"

Her smile is warm, if a little forced.

"George? Didju have a nice flight?"

She Aussie-cheek-kisses me, and I American-hug her. It's awkward. Like foreign policy.

"Yeah, not too bad. A little long, from Panama."

"You must be shattered, being so tall. We'll getchya set up for a kip at the house."

"I'm afraid to nap or else I'll never wake up. But I'd kill for some caffeine? Maybe a jump in the water, if it's easy?"

"'Course. In Bronte? It's nearly impossible to stay dry. Nine minute walk in any direction should meetchya needs."

"My kind of place."

She drops a genuine smile. She is beautiful, even with the heavy eyes of sorrow.

I shift the weight of my carry-on and feel PJ's cremains settle. Now, I'm the one with the forced smile.

We walk out to her car, me accidentally following her to the driver's side.

"Didju want to drive?"

"Ha, no. Habit. Sorry. But let me get the door for you, while I'm here."

It's almost Christmas, and the sun is blinding from the midday summer heat.

I drop my gear in the back and fall into the front seat.

"Jesus, that ozone layer depletion thing is no joke. Damn the sun is strong."

"You reckon?"

"Uhhh…"

"Just teasing, love."

She flips on the air conditioning. I almost drool.

"Why dontchya pop the seat back and rest yah eyes a bit?"

I do.

I doze before she pays the parking attendant.

•

I wake as we crest a hill. A massive park opens up, with an ocean view.

"Wow."

"Not bad, ay? That's Centennial Park. We're almost home."

"Incredible. It looks like a postcard, without having to crop out all of the trash at your feet."

"Central America it's not. True. And you'll be reminded of that when you buy a ten dollah IPA."

Talking about drinking beer within the first hour of meeting? It's confirmed; she's PJ's sister. I want to tell her this. To hear her laugh. But I don't know how to do it.

She pulls over and starts pointing.

"Look. Murray Road. The house. The beach. Coffee. Go straight over that hill and you'll run into Bondi road—take a right and you'll walk straight to the shop."

We park.

"You live here?"

"Pretty flash, eh?"

"Yeah, I just figured…"

"That my brothah dressed like a bloody bogan, so we'd live in a shack?" Bogan = white trash.

"Kinda? He really didn't wear a shirt that much, and when he did it was always one of the ones you guys made for him."

"Oh, PJ. He barely spent a minute in the shop without sneaking off to have a surf!" She giggles, but the tears follow. "I'm so glad yah're here, George. PJ could not stop talking about you. And with you here, it…it…it just feels right, you know?"

"I do."

She leans in for a hug, before her third tear falls.

"Ooof. Whattah mess I am. Come on. Let's getchya settled in."

She shows me my room and then runs to blow her nose.

I drop my backpack on the bed and pull PJ's ashes out. I've wrapped them in a few of his signature t-shirts. The cremains are intact—sealed in a simple but craftsman-made wood urn; it's Panamanian mahogany from a neighboring village. Tsvika, our other roommate, has good taste.

Licking my lips gives me a taste of my gnarly travel breath. I pull out my toothbrush and head to the bathroom. Turning on the faucet, the extravagance hits me.

Pure, clean water. From the tap. No need for filters. No need to lug bottled water from the bodega. Opulent. Just pull the handle and watch it spill out into the sink. I dip my head and take a man-sip. In much of Panama, this act is inadvisable.

I drink and drink and drink.

A thorough tooth-brushing and I feel like a new man.

Time to hand over the urn.

I remove each of the t-shirts I used to protect it and pause on one: *Walkabout—Australian for Homeless Drug Addict.* I stash it for myself and refold the others.

Suzanne is still in her room. Good time to sneak out. I leave the urn and t-shirts on the kitchen counter. Seeing both will crush her. She doesn't need her houseguest witnessing her tears twice in the same day.

I can't help but smile at the topmost t-shirt: *To do list—stop dating bartenders.*

I quietly close the gate behind me and put my sunglasses on.

•

Suzanne's directions are nails. In ten minutes, I'm in a beachy cove, with pounding surf and lounging sunbathers. Bronte beach is Laguna Beach meets La Jolla meets perfection.

Yelp told me that there's a pool at the southern edge, just out of sight of Bronte beach. But the surf is overhead, and my self-loathing is hungry for a beating.

Part of me wants to lie down on the warm sand, fry my skin to a crisp and sleep until I never wake up. But I can't.

I often rock a Speedo under my shorts as underwear. But today, the travel has me beat. I kick off my flip-flops, yank my sweaty shirt over my head and jump in, happy to get some salt water on my travel-filthy shorts. PJ told me about the strong rip currents. I can feel them. I keep my head down and stroke, stroke, stroke till I'm outside the set waves.

Catching my breath, I tread water and take in the surfers and stunning view.

A chiseled Aussie knee-paddles out to me, wearing a Bronte SLSC (Surf Life Saving Club) rash guard.

"You a'right, mate?"

"Yeah, I'm great, thanks."

"Thought you might've gotten caught in the rip."

"Apologies. I know coming out through the rip was a rookie move. I wanted the extra workout. I actually teach swimming, but thanks for looking out for me."

"Canadian?"

"American. Do I sound Canadian?"

"Nah. The Canucks? They get the shits when you call 'em Yanks. It's always safah to guess Canadian first."

"That's hilarious."

"You teach swimming?"

"A little. I grew up doing it, to pay for school."

"Well, we have the Nippahs every Sunday, and we can always use a hand."

"Nippers?"

"We teach the kiddies to swim."

"Ah, gotcha. Very cool."

"Cheers." He turns back toward shore.

Everyone here is nice. And beautiful. And they teach the kids to swim. Under different circumstances, I might move here.

•

"Georgie!"

A fatter, shaved head version of PJ nearly breaks my ribs with a hug. PJ's brother has the swagger of a chubby mob boss being massaged by a supermodel. And, like PJ, the ice-cream-melting Bradley Cooper eyes.

My shorts are still soaked.

"Craigo?"

"Feel like I've known you fah ages. Fancy a drink?"

One of the bottles of Grey Goose is open. Smelling it on his breath, I'm glad I upgraded.

Suzanne is smiling, but her eyes are tear-swollen. Based on the damage that they've done to the bottle, Craigo must've gotten here the minute I left.

Before I have the chance to say yes, Suzanne turns and pulls ice from the freezer. Bending down, I glance at her muscular legs. We're having a tribute to my dead best friend, and I'm checking out his sister's calves.

She hands me a stiff vodka cranberry, and I down half of it in a gulp.

The jetlag hits. I feel a boozy, sleepy tide wash over me. Suzanne and Craigo have unfolded PJ's t-shirts. They're surrounding the urn in a weird hipster shrine.

I read each shirt, one by one. Suzanne matches my mood by playing some bass-heavy house music and refilling my drink.

I saunter around the t-shirts, recalling PJ donning this one in the Panama sun: *If you're not funny, don't talk.*

Seeing them, I rethink hoarding: *Walkabout—Australian for Homeless Drug Addict.*

"There's one more. I'm…I'm sorry. I kept it. One sec."

I run up to my room, throw on dry pants and yank the shirt from underneath my clothes in the closet.

"If it's OK with you guys, I'd like to keep this one?"

"'Course, love."

"Mate, you can have'em all. Especially that one. That one's not even clevah!"

"Yeah…but I disagree. It's obvious, sure. Maybe that's why I like it. It's mindless and fun. It just…it just reminds me of PJ. Everything about him. Confident. Irreverent. Whimsical."

"He was a bit of a poof, wasn't he?"

We laugh. I'll never tell them he called me a *poof*, as he died, bleeding in my arms. We drink. And cry. And talk about fortunes lost in t-shirts.

Suzanne puts my drunk ass to bed. I pass out, nodding off to the sound of Craigo finishing the vodka downstairs. By himself.

•

I wake to the sound of bird mating calls. Goddamn they are loud. And goddamn, I could sleep for a month of Sundays.

On the nightstand, I see that Suzanne left me a glass of water and a sleeve of Berocca—the sworn Aussie hangover cure. A small, sweet gesture from a veteran partier.

I walk downstairs and see a note from her, held down by a spare house key:

*Georg(i)e—*

*Left for work. Favoloso opens at 7. Try one of their ham & cheese croissants. Back at 6. Go for a swim, or pop by the shop—Craig(o) will be there all day.*

*Sx*

At first glance, I read Sx as Sex, not her intended abbreviation of: *Suzanne* with a (friendly) kiss. I'm an idiot. And need to check myself. But I do appreciate her subtle grace of itemizing Craigo and my nicknames.

A quick shower, rehydrating with delicious showerhead water, and I'm out the door.

True to Suzanne's orientation, I find the coffee shop, Favoloso, within four blocks.

"Hi. May I have two macchiatos with an extra shot in each?"

"Two strong machs. Fah here or takeaway?"

"Here. Thanks."

"Both fah you?"

"Yep."

"Just gonna smash'em back?"

"Yeah, jetlag."

"Canadian?"

"Nope. States."

He opens a gallon of milk. He looks like a heavily freckled Ryan Gosling. And I must be right.

"Gosso!"

"Whaaaht?"

"Use the milk that's already out!"

"A'right, a'right."

He returns it to the fridge.

"Did he just call you Gosso, because of Ryan Gosling?"

"Not you too, mate."

"Sorry. But it's not the worst nickname in the world. I'm George."

"Nicholas. But everyone calls me…"

"Gosso."

"Welcome to Sydney, Georgie."

"Does anyone in Australia keep their God-given names?"

"Why bothah?"

"Fair."

A bird cackles outside, as he hands me the first drink.

"Did you hear that?"

"Ay?"

"The bird? The sinister sounding one? They nest outside my room."

"Must be the Magpies. They're always jabbering on."

•

Continuing with Suzanne's directions, I walk directly into Bondi Road. I pass two-dozen friendly, sculpted pedestrians on their way home from a run, a swim or a healthy breakfast. It reminds me of LA, without the plastic surgery. And the awful nasally voices.

The family business is right on the strip. Novelty t-shirts are their mainstay, and the store is aptly named: We've Gotchya Back. They also sell towels and touristy bric-a-brac. A full-sized orange dune buggy guards the doorway.

"Georgie!"

"Hey, Craigo."

"Didjya have a nice sleep?"

"Incredible. Ten hours."

I run my hands along the roll-cage of the buggy.

"This thing is awesome."

"Yeah, the Moke? Bit of a mascot."

"Moke?"

"Means donkey. But it's really a modified Mini Coopah. Can't believe you've nevah seen one."

"It looks like a Jeep procreated with a golf cart. But better."

A few tourists stroll in. I walk around the Moke. There's a decal on the bumper: *Moked? Stoked.*

"My cheeky brotha came up with that. Good one, ay?"

"Solid."

He motions me to the back room, where they print the shirts. It's the perfect man cave: couch, flat screen, high-end iMac and a fridge full of Coopers Ale. He opens four beers and sets two next to me.

"You evah use a silkscreenah?"

"No, but I'm game to try." I pause and look down at the shirt in progress: *Food Swings.* "Craig. Sorry. Craigo. I've gotta say something. It's driving me insane. I've already been here almost two days now."

"Georgie, you've only just landed."

"You don't understand. PJ. I could've…"

"Ah, don't start with that again."

"But it's my…"

He palms my chest. The gesture silences me.

"Give it a rest. My brothah's dead. And I love him. May the horny little wanker rest in peace. But PJ was always a risk takah. The biggest waves. The girl with the meanest boyfriend. He was nevah gonna live forevah. You think you could've stopped it? Caught in the crossfiyah of gun traffickahs? And you a skinny bartendah and bloody poof love advice columnist wanna play supahman? Have a real go."

He has a point. It does sound absurd.

I did try to save PJ's life. I did.

And I also helped him get shot in the first place.

We both grab our beers. One drowning his sorrow, the other his guilt.

"Two things: I like a man that opens two beers apiece. It shows foresight. The first one always goes down too quick. You don't want to wait for the second."

"Agreed."

He crushes (smashes back?) his second and heads toward the fridge.

"Second thing: clothes."

"There's a room full of 'em ten metahs away. Take whatevah you like."

"No, no. I need clothes for the service, not a t-shirt that says: *Bondi, James Bondi* and 007 with a beach ball."

"Didju just make that up?"

"Yeah?"

"Not bad. We'll make a batch tomorrow and see if they sell. You can silkscreen'em yahself."

He jots a note down and mumbles.

"James…Bondi…Keep 'em comin', Georgie. You can earn yah keep."

"So, PJ's service…"

"Undahstood. Suzanne's old bloke is coming. Lance. He's a tall fucko, like you. We'll have 'em pack an extra jacket and trousahs for yah."

"That'd be great. Thanks so much."

"No worries. Up yah bum."

And down goes beer number three.

"Hey, so the Moke?"

"Yeah?"

"You ever drive it?"

•

Craigo and I burn the rest of the day swapping PJ stories, drinking too much, brainstorming t-shirt ideas and folding a new shipment of their signature t-shirts, bulk printed in China. *We've Gotchya Back* is printed, you guessed it, on the back. I'm convinced that Craigo is my surrogate Aussie brother. We're both addicted to weak puns and wordplay. Plus, he sent me home with a shirt. I feel like an actual employee.

The hill up Bondi Road is steep and sobering, which is what I need. I'm thankful for the shirt. I have it wrapped around my neck, as a sun guard. I was hoping to hit another pool on the way home, but my sixth beer nixed that.

Opening the back door, silence and cool air great me. Like a kid late for curfew, I'm happy Suzanne isn't home to see me drunk at 3pm. Even though I'm twenty-nine, I'm not immune to being deferential to my buddy's older sister. Especially since I have a little crush on her.

A quick shower and I fire up my laptop.

Shawna.

---

**From:** Shawna B.

**To:** Georgeous

**Subject:** Marco…Polo?

Hey you—

I miss you.

Can you please send me a one liner and let me know that you got there safe?

I know that you are dealing with a lot, and PJ's funeral is tomorrow. Or is it today? The time change is so confusing.

I would love to hear from you.

Love,

Shawna

PS I'm sorry I have a vagina and therefore prefer being in contact over radio silence.

PPS Fuck that. I'm not sorry.

---

I should respond to her.

And I should respond to TR.

Or? I could procrastinate and review my assignment queue.

Done.

*The Road Less Traveled* lived on my mom's bookshelf. Even though I know neither of my parents read it, they both embodied its core message (at least until the divorce): do the hardest things first.

No thanks.

Millennials do the easiest thing first. Because we're lazy? No. Because we're smart. Doing one easy thing is way better than doing nothing at all. Nothing at all is what people have been doing for generations. That's why everything is so fucked up.

For me, the easiest thing is always my *Esquire* homework.

*Esquire* has a submissions portal for the writing staff. I've been a Staff Writer for a week, and I love saying it. Staff Writer Staff Writer Staff Writer. Most of the staff submit through a text editor, similar to Microsoft Word with a *Send* button. The submission goes first to their section editor and then onto the legal department for review. That way, nothing gets online or, god forbid, into the print magazine before at least two rounds of approvals.

@AskEsquire is new. There's no review cycle. It sits in a queue like a batter's box, then goes straight out into the Twittersphere on a schedule. That will change someday, when editors and lawyers can work at the speed of the Internet.

The result: I'm very careful about what I submit. And I always give myself enough time to make a last minute change.

Scrolling through the submissions, there are hundreds.

I get bored of everyone's love advice curiosity and let my eyes wander around the room. They land on a photo of the Three Musketeers at the beach. PJ, shirtless, as always, looks like he's fresh from the water. Suzanne and Craigo are a little more sun-exposure aware—real adults. It's a guess, but the photo looks pretty recent. It must have been their last fandango, before PJ took off on his walkabout.

And Suzanne.

It's unfair that I get to look at her in a bikini. A privilege that was not earned.

I snap myself out of it and get back to work.

Scrolling through the Tweets, an obvious one bubbles to the top.

*@militantdogdad i can't help it. i fantasize constantly about my best friend's sister. she's perfect! does that make me a bad person?*

*@AskEsquire Not a bad person. But maybe a bad friend.*

The more flippant my responses, the more I know I'll have to rewrite them. Because I know I'm addressing myself.

I would like to have underlined *friend*, but that's not an option. And all caps is a major no-no in the *Esquire* Submission Guidelines.

The back door opens.

"Georgie? You heyah?"

Suzanne, Craigo, PJ—all the same parents. All have strong accents. But each one is different. PJ's sounded chilled out, Craigo's has a tinge of biting wit and Suzanne's is like…

I'd say it sounds like a song, but that's overkill. It's more like a simple melody. Elegant. Efficient.

I close the monitor and involuntarily straighten the framed photo.

"I'm here!"

"Hey."

"Didju have a good day at the shop, Georgie?"

"Yeah, I…"

"I'm sorry. I'm sure you hate that, George."

"Nah, it's fine. PJ, he…"

"Yeah, every email he sent was all about 'Georgie'. It stuck."

"No, no. I like it."

"Ah, OK. Good. But fah the record, I bloody hate Suzie, so…"

"Noted. Suzanne."

We both laugh. It's the laugh of: I'm your houseguest. And I may have gotten your brother killed. I flew a long way to get here. And I miss him. Also, I am intrigued by you.

She pulls drink fixings from the fridge.

I put my hand over the top of the glasses.

"Can I do that? You're making mojitos, right? I could make a dozen in my sleep."

"But yah're the guest!"

"Take a seat."

She hesitates briefly, then takes a seat at the kitchen counter.

She watches me for a moment. Then reaches for a Post-it pad and click pen. Every flat surface in the house has this little combo. She starts drawing, in quick masterful strokes.

I finish making our drinks. Mojito tip: over-crush the mint and under-dose the sugar.

"Are you drawing the edge of this cutting board?"

"The shadows a bit."

"Wow, I'd never have thought the rendering of a block of wood could look so…alive."

"Just a nervous habit, love."

I serve.

"Let me know if it's not sweet enough.

"Oh my god. Delicious. Give us anothah!"

"Thank you. I have tried to do a lot of things well in my life. Unfortunately, the result has been a lackluster writing career and decent drink making. We all have our talents."

"Cheers!"

"Cheers."

We both take big sips: professional self-medicators.

I'm not sure how this is going to go, but now is as good of a time as any.

My hands nervously stir our second round. I need to concentrate. Drinking all day with Craigo has given me a shampoo-effect buzz.

Fuck it.

"Sooo, Charlotte?"

"Yeah?"

"Tsvika. He told me. The probate attorney. He…"

"Ahhh, right."

She accepts her drink refresh and brings it directly to her lips.

"It's not the bird; it's the bloke."

"Huh?"

"That wants the money. Veronica cashiered at the shop fah a few months, before taking a cocktail job. She's a big girl. She knew what she was getting into with PJ. I mean, come on. Who starts shagging a guy that's leaving on a walkabout two weeks latah?"

"A female emotional force field does not exist that PJ could not penetrate."

"And penetrate he did, the little wank."

Her own wit softens her. She finishes her drink.

"She's fine. It's him. Her new bloke. He's pushing her to go aftah the money."

"Ohhh. That makes sense. If it's PJ's daughter…"

"Georgie, our family is so tiny. I'm ecstatic to be her auntie. To know that PJ was a fathah…of course we'd take care of her."

"So you have confirmed that she is PJ's daughter? Blood tests?"

"Whathavyah got a hero's complex or something? Come to sort out yah old roomie's affaiyahs? Of course we did a bloody blood test!"

"I'm sorry. You're right. It's not any of my…"

She sighs. Chews on her outburst for a moment.

"No, I'm sorry. You have every right. You were his best mate. It's just Philip. The thought of being tethered to him forevah is not appealing."

"Philip?"

"Charlotte's mum's bloke. He's a coppah. A real man's man."

"Maybe after PJ, she was looking for someone a bit more stable?"

"Judge fah yahself. He'll be at the funeral tomorrow."

# 2

If I had a dollar for every time I turned on a computer drunk and wished I hadn't—I'd have enough money to buy a computer with a breathalyzer.

Shawna wants to iMessage.

---

George?

Hey.

Hi!

I'm a little drunk, sad and
jetlagged. Sorry.

I figured. I just wanted
to know that you are alive.

Totally. I should have
reached out sooner.
I'm sorry.

I'm not trying to be passive aggressive.
I just miss you. I wanted to hear
your voice.

No, no. I get it.
And I appreciate it.
I really do.

Really?

Shawna…

George, you are so totally fine
alone, by yourself…it drives
me insane.

I'm not trying to be aloof.
I swear. PJ's funeral is
tomorrow, and apparently

the future stepdad is a real
prince. It's giving me anxiety.

That sucks. Your typical
snarky understatement suggests
that he must be a dick.

Who knows. I'm probably
overreacting. PJ's sister said
it as a throwaway comment.
It's just been bugging me.

That must be hard on you.
PJ was your one true committed
relationship. Not said with sarcasm.
Said with reverence. Normally, I
wouldn't wish your daily sharpened
tongue on my worst enemy, but feel
free to use your powers for evil, if
he's that bad.

There she is. You are really good
at validating my mean side. Really
good. And timely. Thank you. Also
not said with sarcasm. Supporting
the dark arts is your love language.

One of them.

Be nice.

Dead serious. I am very
appreciative. I'm not one for pep
talks, but apparently I needed this one.
I hate how there's no context in text.
And don't take that as an opportunity to
push emojis.

You're welcome.

On a lighter note, their family
shop is named: We've Gotchya Back.
They have shirts, and they're only
printed…

On the back???

Bingo.

Love!

Indeed. So sharp.
Does anything ever get

by you?

Yes. You. Literally.

Uhhh…

Never mind.

No, no. It's fair. I'm just…
I'm just a little gun-shy, when
it comes to us. It feels more difficult
than it should be. I know I am part
of that. For sure. A big part of it.
But the sentiment still stands. And
it paralyzes me in a way. Makes me
indecisive. And trust me, your phrase,
"indecision is decision" is not lost on me.

Love love love having my
words used against me.
Your bionic memory hasn't
always been my favorite.

Bionic memory rebranded:
good listener? ;)

George. Seriously.

I thought it was a compliment?!

It was. You jerk.

Legit laugh.

Can I say one thing?

Always.

Just consider us. Consider
it. A lot has happened. If I
know anything about you, it's
that conflict makes you flee.

Ouch.

It's true. But it's not judgment.

Yeah…

Can you just pretend to imagine
a world where we were less…
contentious?

Pretend?

Don't be difficult. I'm only asking you to imagine. Don't tell me you can't commit to that.

OK. OK.

We have something. And you know it.

I know we do.

Is it messy? Yes. But it's worth it. To me, it's worth it. Just say OK.

OK?

Just say OK that you're not 0%. I know I've lost you. I do. But I also know that part of us is written in the cosmos.

Shawna…

Just wait. It's OK. I can let you
go. But admit that it's not 0%.

I believe in math but not
this kind. Do I love you? Yes.
Will I always love you? Yes.
But this benchmarking our
viability is nuts. I'm not putting
a number on us and then being
held to it. I don't know how to
give you what you want and also
be honest and not be misleading.
Do you understand that?

I do. And it's OK. You didn't
say 0%. That's all I wanted.

You with the numbers. Jesus.

I'm good. I love you. I'm
gonna go look at your poolside
Facebook photos and get myself
off. Bye George.

Bye Shawna.

---

And she's gone. You'd think a more drawn out goodbye would be apt, but Shawna knows when to put the shoes in the box, once she's made the sale.

•

4am.

The day of PJ's funeral. Hungover, tired and awake.

The creepy birds don't help. Do they ever sleep?

"Aaaght, aaaght, aaaght, aaah."

It's the least harmonious avian mating call on earth.

I may as well work.

My laptop fires up, with the brightness of a thousand suns.

---

**From:** Lewis, George

**To:** Rogers, Timothy

**Subject:** Sorry for the delay

Tim—

Apologies, I should have written you a day or two ago. I'm still getting my bearings here.

IT has me all set up on the Tweets, and you are the first recipient of my official employee email. I will not lie; it's pretty exciting.

The sheer number of folks writing in is daunting. It's both a blessing and a curse. There's lot of material and, therefore, a lot of material…

One quick work thing: I've been posting in the Esquire Digital portal. Since you are my direct supervisor, please don't hesitate to preview my work before it hits the Twittersphere. I promise to always post a minimum of two days early. And yes, I've read and reread the Esquire Publishing Guidelines.

Regarding flowers/donation: you are too kind. The Ferdinands family asks that donations be made to the Bronte or Bondi Surf Life Saving Club (SLSC). The SLSC is the YMCA here. Watersports are a way of life in Australia and possibly a religion. PJ's brother, Craig, has a daughter in their Sunday class. It's a much better gift than flowers. Regardless, I'm personally touched by Esquire's gesture. It is very kind and very appreciated. I'll forward the donation website to Lydia, under separate cover.

I'll check back in with you in a few days.

Best,
George

---

4:30am here on Sunday is Saturday at lunchtime in New York. Hopefully, TR is bundled up, hitting golf balls off Chelsea Pier. The last thing I need is TR asking for my exact return date.

I try to fall back asleep.

I'll be at church in five hours.

•

7:25am.

The motherfucking birds.

I feel like I slept thirty seconds.

I sit up, pop the computer lid and recheck the hours at Favoloso.

7am to 5pm.

Victory.

I throw on a hat and sneak out. The weather is magic—crisp, but still warm enough to be in shorts.

Gosso is setting up the outside seating with his boss.

"Georgie!"

"Mornin' Gosso."

His boss smirks at Gosso's ubiquitous nickname.

"Didju meet…"

"Mr. Bossman?"

"Yeppers. I'm Mr. Bossman. Howdju know? Nice tah meetchya, Georgie."

"Why is it Georgie and not Georgo, like everyone else?"

"Because Georgo sounds like Joe Joe, and that's what we serve here. Come on inside, and let's make you one."

The birds chime in, with their nasty vowels.

"Aaaght, aaaght, aaaght, aaah."

"Did you hear that?"

"What?"

"That sound! The Magpies. Doesn't it drive you insane?"

"The Magpies? That?"

"Yes! Listen."

We wait ten seconds.

"Aaaght, aaaght, aaaght, aaah."

"That! It actually sounds like the word 'that'! Did you hear it?"

"'Course. But 'that's' not a magpie."

"Really?"

"Who toldja that?" But he already knows. "Gosso! You call yahself an Australian? But you don't even know the difference between a bloody magpie and a bloody raven?"

"You sure it's not a Magpie?"

"Mate. Whattah they teaching you at uni? A stupid little magpie is not gonna make a sound like that."

I can't resist.

"You mean like 'thaaat'?"

"Even the Yank's gettin' cheeky with yah. Georgie, I like yah work."

•

I exit my two coffee shop buddies and their welcome comic relief.

Carrying a piccolo, basically a mini-latte, I secretly hope Suzanne is still snoozing and that I can drink it, while it's still hot.

Nope.

Suzanne pulls her car into the driveway.

If I've learned anything from bartending, it's knowing the face of someone that just hooked up and is embarrassed about it. Suzanne is wearing it like a steel dog collar.

"G'day! Yah're up early!"

"Yeah. Jetlag. Brought you a piccolo. Hopefully you don't prefer almond milk?"

Handing it to her, I pull two sugars from my pocket.

"Aren't you a doll."

She looks tired. And not in the ugly way. In the lonely way. I wonder where she spent the night.

"Pop 'round the side and give us a hand?"

The sports coat and slacks I asked to borrow are hanging on a hook behind the passenger seat. I grab them, and we walk in together, looking like a couple.

•

Showered, shaved and wearing a borrowed suit, I've still got time to kill. I knock out a quick Tweet for work. Poor Charles Dickens, he should've negotiated payment by the character, not the word.

*@bananarepublican my bro sez that being a pallbearer is like being a groomsman at a wedding, super ez to hook up. is that true?*

*@AskEsquire Possibly. Women are communal beings and seek connection during ceremonies. But be careful. Else, you might be attending your own funeral.*

Hmmm. This feels like I'm letting him off the hook. A quick rewrite:

*@AskEsquire False. Capitalizing on raw emotions is predatory and gross. Grieve. Then find a mate elsewhere.*

•

The blown up photo of PJ on the mantle at St. Anne's Catholic Church looks absurd. Juxtaposed next to Jesus, he looks like a modern version of the Messiah, sponsored by Rip Curl.

Due to the gunshot wound, PJ was cremated. But, if he hadn't been, I would've lobbied for his casket attire to be his signature uniform—shirtless, wearing tattered board shorts.

I view the ceremony through a cry-drunk haze. My lips don't tremble. I remain stoic, poised. But damn, the tears fall.

"And now may he lay to rest. Yet, may Peter James Ferdinands remain in our hearts…forever."

Amen, you squirrelly little fucker.

# 3

I have no idea of PJ's ancestry or what to expect culturally post-funeral, but the wake at Casa Ferdinands transitions from: *Where shall we set this casserole?* to: *Where shall we set up the DJ?* Suzanne has shed the sadness and has transitioned into party hostess.

"Georgie, could I trouble you to set up the bar, until Craigo arrives with the meat tray?"

"Absolutely. I can stay there all day."

She gives me an appreciative side hug. I wish it could last a moment longer.

But here they come.

I start setting up the bar, thankful for the task.

There's a loneliness that comes when you travel by yourself or go out to eat in an unfamiliar town. The sense of despondence is overwhelming. And being surrounded by people makes it worse. Then, as soon as you make friends or connect, it disappears as if it never happened. You fall into a rhythm. You forget the loneliness. But it doesn't escape your demeanor. It hangs on you like an ill-fitting suit jacket. Like the one I'm wearing right now.

"Nice sporty, mate!"

Another disgustingly good looking guy tugs at my lapel. I turn and look eye to eye with him. He's tall. And his smile says something knowing—something I can't place.

"Lance?"

"Yeah, good tah meetchya George. And this is my fiancé, Elizabeth."

"Nice to meet you." I look past Elizabeth for Suzanne's eyes, but they're already locked on the back of Lance's head. Now I know where she spent the night. Handsome fucker. "Thanks again for letting me borrow the jacket. Would you guys like a drink?"

"A man with a plan, nice one. I'd love a Coopahs, and I'm sure my bettah half would like something, wouldn't you, Lizzie? She just flew in from Perth this morning."

She gushes at the attention.

*Hey, Elizabeth, why didn't you have Suzanne pick you up from the airport? She was already up and in her car, and Lance Romance surely needed time to change the sheets.*

"Georgie!" Craigo. A sight for sore eyes. "G'day, Lance, how you going?"

Craigo is polite with Lance, but he maintains an edge and brushes past him, straight toward me. I could kiss him.

"I've got somethin' fah you! But give us a look a bit latah, ay?" He hands me a plastic bag, wrapped around a bottle of Scotch in a box.

I pop three Coopers and hand Craigo his first (sorry, Lance).

"Yah're a legend."

The three of us cheers.

"Pardon my rudeness." Pointing to the cabernet, I nod to Elizabeth. "This cab do for you?"

"Perfect. Thank you."

Craigo taps my shoulder.

"Give us a glass for my girl, ay?"

Fourth drink poured, and more to come, I'm back in the bartending business.

Craigo grabs the hand of a Rubenesque woman of indeterminate age. Twenty? Forty? She's in a deferential black dress, other than it's missing a yard of fabric underneath her neck. Not the dress I would have chosen for a wake, but she pulls it off.

"Georgie, is it? PJ's mate from the States?"

"Hi, yeah…"

"I'm Ava."

"Pleased to meet you." She looks like Adele's alter ego, with a dash of punk rock. She's striking. I'm not alone in noticing. Lance's head swivels so quickly, I think it might snap off. Good luck with that marriage, Elizabeth.

"Ava, would you mind handing this other glass to Suzanne? She's right behind you, a little stuck in conversation."

"'Course."

"Craigo, let me run that up to my room."

"Be careful; it's fragile. And grab some OJ from the fridge on the way back? Hannah isn't old enough to drink Coopahs yet, and you can use it for a mixah."

"Gotcha."

I grab the plastic bag and head upstairs. It's heavy. Scotch. I can see the outline of the Glenlivet emblem on the box. I know he wanted me to save it, but post-funeral, I'm on information overload and wouldn't mind throwing back something stiff. The toothbrush holder in the bathroom as a glass? I've done worse.

I dump out two toothbrushes, give it a rinse and head to my room. I open the box. Not scotch. It's a trophy. *Australia Junior Surfing Titles – 1st Place – Peter "PJ" Ferdinands.*

Fuck.

Tears.

And tears.

And footsteps.

I wipe the snot away.

Suzanne pops her head in. Her glass of wine nearly gone.

"I told him not to give you that today. Sorry, love."

"No, no. I'm appreciative. Are you sure you guys don't want to keep it?"

"There's a closet full of them at the shop. Take ten more with you."

A laugh. And more tears.

She leans down and wipes one off my cheek.

I stand up and hug her.

And she lets me.

We hug. Maybe a little too long.

She taps out.

"We should go. You a'right?"

"Yeah, yeah, good. Thanks. Should get back to the bar anyway."

"You reckon? Surely Ava and her tits are due fah another drink."

"Are they not insane?"

"Careful not to stare too long, they'll burn into yah retinas and give you cata-racks. Get it?"

"Got it. Craigo's vibe is…"

"A full figured woman? Bit of a fetish. Both my mum and I are so boyish, he went the other way. You should see Hannah's mum."

"Curvy?"

"You'd need a ute just to get her out of the grocery store." Ute = Utility Vehicle = SUV.

"Interesting. More power to him."

"He'll need it, if he evah wants to pick Ava up and carry her ovah the threshold."

"Are we being nice? And if we're picking on better halves, didn't you used to date Lance Romance?" I regret it, as soon as I say it.

"How kind of Craigo to mention that to you."

"Sorry. I just…he's not even in your league. Not even close." I couldn't be more sincere. But her face takes it as half-flattery. That's OK. I deserve to be half-understood.

"Lance? He's a good guy. Just a bit…well it doesn't mattah. Plus, he's an absolute peach compared to Philip. Just wait. He's downstairs. Come on, let's go."

She grabs my hand and pulls me for a few steps before letting go. I turn, see the plastic gold of the trophy, and hear PJ's voice: *Are you trying to bloody shag my sistah, mate?*

•

Downstairs, I spot him in a millisecond.

Philip.

He's beefy, with that close-cropped hair that's all the rage now. Except that his looks like it was done by a trainee at Supercuts. He's vaping. It seems like a trashy thing to do at a wake. A Kindle will never fully replace a paperback, even though it's way more efficient, and an electronic cigarette will never look as cool as a legit cigarette. But I must admit, as a swimmer, I much prefer vapes to millions of cigarette butts littering our waterways.

Still, he reminds me of the tactless prison guard, Pornstache, from *Orange is the New Black.*

And there's little Charlotte. Picture perfect. Her tiny mouth is cooing, but it's too loud to hear her. Incredibly docile, given the surroundings. I didn't hear a peep from her at the funeral.

And her mom.

She sees me looking at her and smiles. Drops her guard for a moment.

Her tasteful grey pashmina falls. Just for a second. She grabs it with the quick hands of shame or someone withholding a secret they don't want to keep. It breaks my heart a little.

"Hi. I'm George."

I'm addressing her, but he answers.

"Ah, the American! Or as we say here—Americunt!" He laughs and sucks on his vape. Suck my dick, motherfucker.

PJ's baby mama smiles apologetically.

"Hello, I'm Veronica."

"Nice to meet you. And this must be Charlotte. Wow. She's gorgeous. Mind if I hold her? I literally just washed my hands."

"Sure. Just be careful of her head."

"Absolutely."

Even though she's swaddled up, I hold her like a loaf of bread without a bag—careful that the last two slices don't slide down my leg.

"Have you got her for a moment? I'd love to use the loo."

"Yeah, go for it. I'm good."

Charlotte's teeny baby's breath smells divine. No wonder they named a flower after it.

"Such a treat to use the toilet by mahself."

Veronica smiles and turns, but Philip barks.

"Vee!"

He points to his empty beer, and she nods in compliance.

It's official—I hate this guy.

I bounce Charlotte and walk her around the party. The wake that feels like a party. I'd bet money that PJ's distant cousin is hooking up in the bathroom. Charlotte is warm. And calm. I have to remind myself that we're at her father's funeral. Walking around with her makes me wonder how long I'll be chased by PJ's ghost.

Veronica hands Philip a beer. He grabs it and doesn't even glance at her. Prick. She can feel my eyes on her, as she walks back. If I was going to make her a t-shirt for Christmas, it'd be: *Don't judge. I don't have a lot of options.*

"Yah're a natural with her."

"It's not hard; she's asleep. And infants gravitate toward immaturity. I've got that in surplus."

Philip watches us, wondering if I'm threatening his alpha male status. But Veronica knows not to linger too long, with her dead baby daddy's bestie.

"Here, let me take her."

"Thanks for letting me hold her. And let me know if you're taking applications for godfather."

"Yah're sweet. I don't think there'll be a lot of competition."

# 4

"You hadja chance, why didn't yah run?"

"Huh?"

"When you were holding Charlotte?"

"Ah. Yeah. I actually thought about it. What the fuck is up with Philip Morris?"

"The macho culture is a bit more ingrained here than in the States."

"And his last name is LeCompte, mate."

"Philip Morris the tobacco company. Nickname. I was trying to fit in."

"Ahhh. You sure you were PJ's mate? PJ was not one for quips."

"Because he lived playfulness; he didn't need to create it."

"Jesus, Georgie. Don't go all existential."

Suzanne sets an open bottle of wine and three glasses on the table. We're having the wake post mortem. The after party. The house is destroyed.

"I'm gonna stick with beer. Craigo?"

"Nice one. And toss us Hannah's blankie, ay?"

Quiet little Hannah is passed out on Craigo's lap. He tucks her in with a Disney *Frozen* blanket.

"Back to Philip Morris. I hate that guy."

Suzanne nestles into the couch, faded.

"Strong words, mate."

"Sorry. I fucking hate that guy."

"He's not a huge Georgie fan, neithah. After he called you a cunt, he added 'yank rhymes with wank,' as soon as you turned yah back. The fuckwit."

"Charming." Suzanne chimes in, even though she looks asleep, with the wine glass resting on her tummy.

"Suzanne, did he evah have a crack atcha?" Crack atcha = did he ever hit on you/ask you out. It's not: *did he ever hit you.* The Aussie slang—it's tricky.

"Nah, but he's made the rounds. Girls talk."

"You've not always had the best taste in blokes, Suze, so…"

"Ah fuck off, Craigo! I'm not gonna get an earful from a bloody chubby chasah!"

"Oh, Suzanne! Goin' fah the throat, ay? Or should I say, goin' fah the double chin!"

I laugh so hard, beer threatens to go up my nose. I'm glad she lashed out. It opens the door for me.

"Craigo, I, too, am curious. You're all about the full-figured ladies, eh?"

"I love a real woman! Not some matchstick that's gonna snap when you get on top of her fah a shag!"

"Your six-year-old daughter is asleep on your lap."

"She's in a coma. It's hours past her bedtime. Plus, we've gotta get up at seven fah the Nippahs. Santa's comin'."

I brought two beers apiece for Craigo and me, and we're both on our second. Suzanne tucks her bare feet underneath my leg. They are freezing. I wince. Craigo watches this transpire, unflinchingly.

She keeps shuffling her feet, to warm them up, and it's massaging my hamstrings—a pleasant byproduct.

"Santa?"

Suzanne sits up, excited, but keeps her feet intact.

"He comes in on a Zodiac, lands on the beach and hands out ice creams to the little Nippah's! Georgie, you have to see it!"

"That's incredible. If I had known Australia was so aquatically oriented, I'd have come here much sooner. But aren't the kids cold after swimming? Ice cream sounds…"

"They're six 'n' seven. They'd eat popsicles in an igloo, if Kris Kringle said it was a'right."

"Fair. I'm in. Sounds amazing."

"We can drop Hannah and hit the shop aftah. Wanna print up yah *Bondi, James Bondi* brainchild."

"Really? That seems like such a waste of time. How many of those could you actually sell?"

I toss a throw blanket over Suzanne. She welcomes it. She sets her wine down on the coffee table and picks up yet another click pen and a Post-it pad. This clutter would drive me crazy, but it suits her. She's so unpretentious about her art. In under twenty seconds, she's drawn a perfect fractal. Tomorrow, she'll write over it with a to do list.

"Mate, the Intahnet is keeeling us. Even we buy our own bulk shirts from China. Our pops made all of his money in real estate—by selling the land and the shop in Melbourne—not in bloody t-shirts and swag."

"Then why do you keep it open? Look at this house. I don't know if you have Zillow down here, but I'm guessing it's worth two million? Clearly you don't need the shop to put food on the table."

"We keep it open because I love it. And, occasionally, if we can print original ideas, they blow out the door lickety split. I'm thinking about expanding into the greeting card business—that's where the real money is."

"Because of the margins?"

"Exactly."

He unbuttons his shirt and takes it off, revealing a t-shirt underneath: *Just because I can't pick you up doesn't mean I don't want to hold you.*

"Can't imagine why some of your t-shirt concepts aren't flying off the shelf. Jesus that is offensive, Craigo."

He smiles wide, prideful.

I point at his shirt for emphasis and return my hand to Suzanne's leg—where I realize that it's been this whole time.

•

1am.

I have to get up at 6:45. But I can't stop cleaning. I've already taken five recycling trips to the alley, and I set each in as quietly as possible.

Suzanne is out. Out.

I open a beer that I know I'll never finish and haul another load out. It feels good to be moving—party cleanups are meditative like that.

I stop and look at Suzanne.

So peaceful.

I decide to leave her there. I'd like to wake her up and tell her to go to bed, but it's not my place. I turn off the remaining lights and set Hannah's *Frozen* blankie over her feet.

Tiptoeing away, her phone dings. Guess who.

Lance: *You up?*

With her eyes barely open, Suzanne rolls over on the couch, toward her phone.

I turn toward the kitchen, pretending I didn't see it.

She leans up on her elbow, looks at it and turns the sound off.

I set the last of the glasses on the kitchen counter.

"Come here, Georgie."

She says it with confidence, knowing I won't decline.

I crawl in behind her, sandwiching myself between her body and the back of the couch. She nestles in. I pull her in tighter with my arm, and she cradles it. For two milliseconds I'm nervous, wanting to kiss her, but every ounce of weight drops out of her. She's back asleep.

The things we do to not have to sleep alone.

•

Suzanne's movement wakes me.

Sunlight. Headache. Chill.

She gets up, yawns and tucks the Disney blanket around me.

"I'm gonna grab some coffee. Why don't you sleep a little more and holstah that thing—it's been sticking in my back fah ages."

I crack one eye open. She reaches down, takes her index finger and outlines my package, grazing my erection in a single motion. If there was ever a recipe for pre-ejaculate…

"Does it evah sleep?"

"Sorry, I uhhh."

"It's a'right love. At thirty, us girls are happy to get any attention at all." It's a lie. And we both know it. She tucks me back in and leaves my penis alone. "Coffee ordah?"

"Two macchiatos. With double shots."

"Gotchya. See you shortly."

"Oh, and some food? Anything. Just something full of butter and toasted?"

"We'll make it two. Ciao."

I'm not hungry, but I ask for food, toasted, for another reason. To buy some time. As soon as the side door shuts, I race upstairs.

This won't take long.

As I speed-masturbate, I pause long enough to take a quick glance at her photo on the desk.

It's shameless.

But it works.

Even with PJ and Craigo watching me.

Thank god I'm an only child. If I'd been PJ, with his sister's friends sleeping over all the time, the incessant autoeroticism might've stunted my growth.

I remove the evidence and take a leisurely shower.

Drying off, I realize what time it is.

"Aaaght, aaaght, aaaght, aaah."

The birds tell me it's already after seven.

Dang it. Nippers.

I can hear Suzanne's footsteps on the stairs.

"Georgie?"

"Hey, can you give me a ride?"

"Yeah, I just remembahed; you've got the Nippah's with Craigo, right?"

"It starts at eight?"

"You should be fine. Plus, they don't really need yah help anyway. But, some of the young female lifeguards are not to be missed in their swimmahs. Grab yah kit. You can go for a propah swim and watch Kris Kringle in all of his glory."

"Perfect."

I throw on a shirt, grab my gear and head downstairs. I'm greeted by the two coffees from the Panama House and some delicious bready thing.

"You complete me."

"Let's go, Romeo."

•

What a scene.

Surf Life Saving is a competitive sport in Australia. It makes sense, given the majority of the population's proximity to the ocean. Countless dads are wearing their Bronte SLSC baseball hats and tucking colored bathing caps onto the heads of the little Nippers.

Hannah does not look ecstatic.

"G'day, mate! Yah're looking a bit average!"

"Ooof. Tough to wake up. But I'll get there. The water will help my headache. What can I do?"

"Nah, nothin'. We've got it covahed. Half of these corporate dads? It's the only parenting they do all week. Why dontchya just watch, have a propah swim and keep an eye out for Santa? He'll come in guns ablazin' at about quarter till."

"Magic."

He points up the boardwalk.

"You see where the blokes are setting up those cones? That's where the Bronte Baths are. Or, as we say, 'the pool'."

"Great. Thank you. See you in a bit. Hannah! I'm gonna watch you, OK?"

"Okaaay." She looks up at Craigo, while holding onto his leg for warmth. "Daddy, it's gonna be sooo cooold."

"You'll be fine, sugah. Look at Georgie. He's goin' in, too." I show her my goggles and smile.

"It'll be so fun! I'll see you when you get up there!"

"A'right Hannah, yah group is forming."

They head toward a pack that's gearing up to do leapfrogs across the sand. Leapfrogs are irrelevant for learning how to swim, but they have to keep the kids busy. Yellow, green, red—all of their little heads bob at each station. It's a bizarre aquatic decathlon for six-year-olds.

Walking up the boardwalk, it's cool to see the little groups and the dads cheering them on. Sixty-pound kids carrying a lifesaving raft a few feet sounds ridiculous, but it's heartwarming to see everyone pursuing a common goal.

The pool.

Flawless. Rugged. Gorgeous. Surreal. Indescribable. I drop my shorts, tie the string on my Speedo, adjust my goggles and walk down the steps.

Ice. Cold.

For some reason, I wasn't expecting it to be freezing. Dumb. It's freezing because it's salt water. Only Americans would think to chlorinate and heat water adjacent to the ocean. Here, it's just a little tamed cove, with the waves crashing against it. The tiled lane lines look like pinstripes on a pair of ripped overalls. Safe and scary at the same time—just how we like it.

I crank some laps and warm up.

Taking a break, I stand up and look for Hannah.

Her pack runs toward the pool. Part of the obstacle course is to swim/walk/hop through the shallow end. They look terrified. It's two feet deep. Hannah is the shortest in her group, but she's still forty inches tall; no one's drowning today.

Hannah pauses at the bottom step and crosses her arms. If it's possible to suffer death by cuteness, I'm done.

"Hannah Amelia Ferdinands, get in that watah!" Craigo sputters out, amongst a torrent of his own laughter. Watching her hobble/dog paddle fifteen feet, as if she's crossing the English Channel, cracks me up too.

"Nice job, Hannah!" I cheer from the edge.

A zero-value-add dad in the pool sucks in a deep breath and submerses himself. I watch him, prepared to get annoyed. Underwater, he swims toward Hannah and then semi-surfaces, making a fake shark fin with his flat palm on top of his head.

"You fucking idiot."

Hannah sees him coming, more curious than scared. I continue talking aloud to myself.

"Don't. Please don't. She's only six."

Zero Dad jumps out of the water, making a shark/bear combo snarl at Hannah.

"RAAAHHRGRRR!"

"AAAHHH!!!! DADDDEEE!!"

The millisecond before Craigo scoops her from the water, he drops his lower jaw and shifts it to the side. A fighter's move. An involuntarily movement to draw in more air, just before striking a blow. Craigo might hit him. I hope so.

"Hahahahah! Gotchya!"

"Nice one. You wank."

Craigo, cradling her, steps out of the pool.

"Afraid of the sharkies, are yah?"

Zero Dad pump fakes another snarl toward Hannah, but she's too buried in Craigo's shoulder to notice.

"Give it a rest, mate."

"Scared of the..."

"Enough!"

Craigo slams his open palm inches from Zero Dad's nose. Message received. Next time, this hand becomes a fist.

"Sorry. Bit of a joke."

"She's six years old. Give it a rest."

The fear in Zero Dad's eyes is transparent.

"Apologies. Sorry. So sorry, mate." His voice trails off. At least he is smart enough to walk away. Hannah continues clinging to Craigo. His eyes follow Zero Dad.

Craigo pulls Hannah's head back, gently, making her look him in the eyes.

"Sweetie. Daddy will nevah let anything happen to you. Nevah, evah. OK?"

Her fearful expression is a heart melter.

"Nevah evah, evah?"

"Nevah evah, evah, forevah."

He kisses her forehead.

Craigo finishes drying her with a towel. A few of the mothers fawn over him from a distance—a lost marketing opportunity for a team of divorce attorneys. Their husbands are checked out, watching the surf or the female lifeguards.

Shrieks.

We have a visual of Santa in the Zodiac. The surf is rough, maybe shoulder-high for the surfers, and Santa is struggling to stay standing.

I towel off and join Craigo.

"Is he gonna make it?"

"If an outside set comes, and wipes out that satchel of goodies, there will be bloodshed."

Hannah jumps up and down.

The speed of her emotional recovery is incredible.

"What's the purpose of the orange buoy ball at the front?"

"That's Rudolph's nose. They had a red one, but a shark nicked it. A real shark." Craigo casts a glance toward Zero Dad's performance location. "Not that fuckwit."

•

9:30am.

I can feel my neck reddening from the sun. Australia is unquestionably owed some carbon credits.

Gosso is behind the counter, and he lights up, ready for me.

"Georgie! Two strong machs?"

"Just one, thanks."

"Ah, you've been up early and had a dip, ay? Nice one."

"Yeah, I saw Santa come for the Nippers. Pretty awesome."

He hands it to me. I set my backpack down and grab a sugar packet.

"Thank you."

"My pleasure. Hey, so how are the birds going? Waking you up?

You've really made me more aware of how bloody annoying they are."

"Every morning. But they are bugging me less and less. I think it's because it sounds like they're asking each other questions, but the answer is always 'no'. Like: "Aaaght, aaaght, aaaght?...Naaah."

He points to my bag of swim gear, on the floor.

"Is thaaat, myyy baaack paaack?...Naaah."

"Wow. Perfect."

"I try my best."

"And everyone says you're just a pretty face."

•

A quick shower and I'm back at the computer. Scrolling through the Tweets, they all become a blur. I procrastinate, checking my emails.

---

**From:** Shawna B.

**To:** Georgeous

**Subject:** Santa Klewis is coming to town?

Hi!

I know how much you hate holiday planning, but I wanted to let you know that my mom invited you to Christmas dinner.

Do you think you'll be back by then?

Holiday planning AND question-asking, your two favorite girl traits.

I should've titled this email 2 for 1.

When we were dating, I was joking when I said my tits were the only two things keeping us together. But maybe I was right ;)

Hope all went well with PJ's thing, and maybe see you under the mistletoe?

Love,

Shawna

PS If you hate planning and questions so much, did you ever think you might just not like girls?

---

After three breakups, an infidelity and a no-strings vacation, I'm reluctant to plan family events with Shawna. I should tell her that—straight up. But, as we've established, I'm not fantastic at taking my own advice.

Suzanne dragging her fingernail the length of my penis earlier is irrelevant.

OK, possibly relevant.

Another scroll through the Tweets and my opportunity to anonymously lash out surfaces. Being passive aggressive feels right.

*@hotelbartab I've been dating a cool girl for two months. She wants me to spend Christmas at her parents' house. Too soon?*

*@AskEsquire Holidays catalyze relationships. For better or worse. Think twice before her grandma knits you a stocking, if it's going to end up full of coal.*

Thank god I have two days to re-review that, when I'm less wired and grumpy. Hopefully adding a silver lining doesn't exceed the character max.

All of the typing makes me look at my hands. The phrase: I *know it like the back of my hand* is debatable, because I sure don't know mine anymore. The scar from the bullet that grazed my wrist is a constant reminder of the other one that landed in PJ's chest.

I should check in with Tsvika, back in Panama, at some point.

---

**From:** Rogers, Timothy

**To:** Lewis, George

**Subject:** Housekeeping

George—

Sorry to bother you post-PJ's services, but I did want to alert you to one thing. Mandatory annual training kicks off in January. It's a nuisance, but it is compulsory. It also must be conducted in person. This includes sexual harassment training (very appropriate, given the topic of your work, my friend), code of conduct review, ethics, etc.

Classes can be taken at the Hearst offices in New York, Chicago, San Francisco or LA. Lydia gave the LA office a heads up that you'll be popping in. Let me know if you'd prefer to come to Manhattan. Personally, that's my preference. It'd be great to catch up in person and talk about the upcoming year, but we can also do that another time. I presume you'll be with your family over the holidays.

Best,

TR

PS Lydia arranged a donation to the Bronte Surf Lifesaving Club. Do share our condolences with PJ's family.

---

My boss. He's so nice; it's painful.

•

I feel like an idiot walking over the hill to Bondi wearing my Beats earphones, but the melancholy playlist suits my mood and takes the edge off the heat. My sunburnt neck is one exposed street corner away from peeling.

Stepping into the crosswalk, I instinctively look the wrong way and walk in front of an oncoming bus.

"Whoa!"

Swinging my right arm around, I jump back onto the curb. My elbow catches the earphone cord, hard.

"Damn. Ow!"

Safely crossing, the shady side of the street feels ten degrees cooler. I stave off skin cancer on my earlobes. Two issues ago, *Esquire* taught me that the ears are one of the most melanoma-prone spots for men. Magazine insights, unlike us humans, will never die.

•

"Georgie!"

"Long time no see."

"What happened to yah arm? I knew my sistah was a bit of a bitah," he clacks his teeth, "but I didn't know she was intah whips."

There's a legit welt on my bicep. That, along with my face blushing, is creating a blood tug of war.

"Uhhh..." I drop my backpack and sit at his desk, in front of the monster iMac. "My earphone cord, it…"

"No worries. I'd much rathah have her shacked up with you than constantly going back to that knob."

"Lance?"

"Whaaaht?"

"Nothing. Never mind."

"Is she steeel doing ovah nights with that fucking wank?" The more pissed he gets, the longer his vowels get.

"She doesn't sound like she has the best track record with men."

"What's that? Mistah footsie?"

Ooof.

"Craigo, look, nothing happened…" He snaps out of it and responds with a sharp smirk.

"I don't give two fucks about my sistah canoodling with you. Yah're a good mate. You both are a bit sad. Whatevah. It's these bloody wanks that string her along. 'I'm gonna marry yah' this and 'what'll our kids look like' that—all the while with another bird on the hook. And not just the hook, with a ring on their bloody fingah!"

Translation: *it's totally cool if you sleep with my sister.*

"Can we get off this topic for a few minutes? I had some ideas…"

"'Course. Sorry to get so heated. She's my only sistah, and I love her."

"I know. I know. I've been hearing about you guys fighting for her honor forever. PJ never had a bad word to say about you two. And to be honest, he really looked up to you."

"Shut it, you cheeky fuckah." He warmly slugs me.

"Ouch. Wrong arm, man."

"Sorry. Meant to hit the othah one. Not where Suzie had you tied up all night. You've been a bad boy, Georgie…"

•

It's nice to be coming home sober for once.

I cross Bondi Road and know that I'm halfway home. It's the third time and already feels like my daily commute. Even in foreign lands, we all seek routine.

Sliding open the back door, the shock of air conditioning feels amazing. Suzanne is snoozing on the couch and greets me sweetly.

"Aftahnoon, love. Nice time with Craigo?"

"Yeah, it was great. For such a meathead-looking guy, he's got layers inside that brain of his, you know?"

"He's my brothah, so I think he's a bit of an idiot. But I know whatchya mean. Nevah a dull moment with Craigo in the mix."

"Did you get a haircut? It looks nice."

She grimaces and runs her fingers through it.

"She gave me newscastah hair!"

She's right. Both sides are symmetrical. It looks like her face is outlined by two parentheses.

"It looks great. Hey, I think I'm gonna go lie down, too. Craigo was on his third beer when I left. But after last night, I'm on the wagon. At least for tonight."

"Sadly untrue. You may take a kip, but yah're back on the sauce tonight. Yah're in demand and need to be in good form."

"Huh?"

"Craigo's girl, Ava. Her band."

"Yeah. I know. He told me. But he said it was black tie. And he said it was optional."

"It is not optional! He's just being polite! Geooorgiiieee…"

"Suzanne, I'm shattered. I drink a lot. And I mean a lot. But even this is too much. Plus, I didn't come here on vacation, and I didn't pack a tuxedo. So it's not happening."

"Look how cute you are when yah're tired! And it's fancy dress, love, not formal dress. Fancy dress means costumes."

"Wow. OK. That makes more sense."

"Didjya really think the lead singer of a band with ginormous breasts falling out of her top doing Amy Winehouse covahs in a bogan bar would have red carpet entry?"

"Fair. Their name, Miss Anne Thrope, says it all."

"Craigo has already texted twice, confirming that I'm coming. That means yah're coming."

"OK, OK. I'm in."

"That's a good boy."

"Can I rummage through the garage to make a costume? What smells like frosting?"

"Bugger!" She jumps up and sprints to the kitchen. "Phew. Perfect. All done."

She pulls a rectangular cookie tray from the oven.

"Cool. Looks like an apartment complex. Or a prison?"

"Exactly! I'm gonna mount it on a cutting board, strap it 'round my neck and voila! Fancy dress complete!"

"Sara Lee?"

"Naaah! Edible Complex!"

"Whoa."

"Get it?"

"Got it."

"I can entice the handsome blokes to have a bite!"

"Speechless."

"Here. I made extra. Eatchya mummy issues away." She slides another cookie sheet toward me. This one is fully frosted, and she dips her finger in and takes a lick.

I shake my head.

"What? You don't have a taste for day-old bread?" She looks at her reflection in the microwave window and taps her forehead, leaving a dab of frosting on her temple.

"You look perfect, and you know it. Don't bait me."

"Then stop taking the bait."

"I love that you never say 'mate' as a transition, even when it tees itself up."

"Intellectual elitism is not a crime, love."

"Speak for yourself." She picks up a cookie and tries to feed it to me, giggling. "Suzanne. You're my best friend's sister. That's just one of many reasons we shouldn't play this flirty game."

"Georgie, I'm not holding you to anything. I know yah're leaving soon." She pauses. Becomes less flirtatious and more sincere. "And PJ said it himself, 'He's such a good bloke, I'd let him date my sistah.'"

"He did not say that."

"He did. Just not to me. To Craigo."

"Whoa."

She starts trimming the apartment complex with a cheese knife.

"Is it yah girl back home?"

"Shawna? No. Weeelll…yes?"

"Good answah. Honest." She taps my chest.

"The whole reason I came here was to become an active participant in my life. To not let my life happen to me. To stop floating from one decision and one place to the next. No more drifting. Including my love life."

"Makes sense. But for a bloke, that'll be nearly impossible."

"I know. I'm not saying I'm a saint. I'm just saying I'm trying. Trying to be better." I pause, wanting to be heard, understood. But even I'm not convinced. "You asked about Shawna. I've never loved anyone more. But I also never admitted to her that I had surrendered to her love. Never told her that she was the one."

"Is she?"

"I dunno. There's so much scar tissue there. It'd take a fully fresh start. I'm not sure if I have the energy for that."

"She was unfaithful?"

"Yeah. And that hurt. But I also know I was partially at fault for that. And that's not all of it. I think I could get over that. It's…it's…everything with her…she's just never satisfied. Or she wasn't. I think that's what hurt me the most. And now that I'm gone, I'm everything she wants."

"I know the feeling, unfortunately."

"I know. It sounds cliché." I look at her, for a quick moment, second-guessing my forthcoming honesty. "She came out to Panama. Well, twice, but once recently. A month and a half ago."

"Oh dear."

"No, it was good. I'd be lying if I didn't admit that I was a bit lonely. But I was also curious. If I'd be pulled back in or closing a chapter."

"That's a long way to travel to close a chaptah. Sounds a bit more like renewing a book at the library."

"Ouch. But true."

"Yah're not alone, darling. I've got a few overdue biographies mah'self."

# 5

Like every other garage on earth, this one is filled to the brim with nothing. Absolutely nothing. I look around and take inventory. Suzanne's clever, twisted costume challenges me to step it up. Edible Complex. Hmmm.

A dusty Baby Bjorn in one of Craigo's piles speaks to me.

Done.

I strap it on. Or at least try to. It takes five tries. How many straps does it take to hold a twenty-pound baby? But it fits. And it's comfortable. And the Bjorn saddle is gonna be a great storage spot for a jacket and/or a spare drink and/or Suzanne's phone.

I prance through the sliding glass door, owning my get-up. I'm holding a stack of Suzanne's old subscription magazines. Forever the ambassador, I've already picked out primarily the Hearst publications. I have an *Esquire* upstairs that I bought at the airport—to fully represent.

Suzanne's subscriptions are a collection of interior design and fashion magazines. With one exception. She has a penchant for tattoo rags.

"Can I have these? I only grabbed the ones that were already ripped."

"Sure. They should all go in the bin, anyway. Whatchya up to?"

I roll the eighth magazine up and pop it into the Bjorn, standing proud of my creation.

"Get it?"

"Nah…"

"It goes with your theme of juvenile neuroses."

"Okaaay?"

"Dang it. I knew it was too weird. Check it: magazines come in issues. Bjorns are worn by fathers. Get it?"

"Uhhh…"

"Daddy Issues!"

"Hmm. Esoteric. And supah fucked up. Supah fucked up. No one will get it. No one. Othah than Craigo, who will love it."

"At least its original? I don't care. It's so comfortable; I'm gonna use it as a purse."

"Keep it on. Plus, even though you won't play in my sandbox, not one of the anime freak sluts will comprehend yah cheeky quip, so I can keep you all to mahself."

"Anime freak sluts?"

"The skinny Chinese girls with their short skirts, tiny twats and ovahplayed Aussie accents. Australia is gonna become the next Taiwan, with us selling all of our mineral rights off by the minute. I've got no empathy for a twiggy two-drink stunnah in a size zero."

"Envy. Hate. Admiration. All synonyms. By the way, anime is Japanese, you racist."

"Judge me now, but trust me, these bitches are so hot, hating them is a form of idolahtry."

"Idolatry. Nationalism—although possibly misguided. Racism. Complex and edible. Damn."

"Tormenting isn't it? You'd best not drink too much tonight, eh love?"

•

One of my favorite times is the downtime before any event. Because you want to spend the time doing something, but you don't have enough time to do anything.

*@salsaslut my gf says she knows i love her but that I don't speak her "love language". WTF?!*

*@AskEsquire Even more than being loved, humans desire to be seen and understood.*

---

**From:** Lewis, George

**To:** Rogers, Timothy

**Subject:** RE: Housekeeping

Tim—

Regarding training—I will be there. Good call on LA. I'd also prefer to come to NYC. It would be great to catch up in person, but I've not seen my mom in a year, and Christmas is her favorite.

Thank you and everyone at Esquire for making the donation to the Bronte SLSC in PJ's name. It was truly a classy touch. And the money is in good hands. I personally witnessed Santa arrive in an aquatic sleigh, to motivate the kids to swim. Pretty cool, eh?

Thanks again, and looking forward to working together more next year.

Best,
George

PS I know you're super hands off, but I have two Tweets in the queue. Would love to know if I'm on the right track, have captured the right voice, etc. But only if you have time.

---

One down, one to go.

---

**From:** Georgeous

**To:** Shawna B.

**Subject:** santa sleighs all the ladies

hey you
please thank your mom for the invite. esquire has me signed up for

training right around christmas, and i might be in new york, so i'll keep you posted. your mom's cooking does sound delicious, regardless.

all is well here. pj's stuff has wrapped up. that is, with the exception of pj's baby mama shacking up with that guy that creeps me out. the guy i mentioned the other day. i can't put my finger on it, but his energy is a bit date rapey.

on the upside, it's been really moving to be here. to see so many people rally to pay tribute to a guy that hadn't worn underwear in three years has been charming and heartbreaking. plus, craigo and suzanne's hospitality is ridiculous (it runs in the water here). they treat me like family and even have me running errands for the family business.

will let you know when my plans firm up.

g

ps trying to keep a separation between church and state on the emails. hope that's cool.

---

Stop judging. Here are the top five reasons I lied to Shawna:

1. Sometimes, lying is just easier.
2. Committing to Christmas dinner would not quell the question asking and planning; it would multiply it by ten. For example: *My mom wants to know if you like cranberries? Are you gonna sleep over? Do you want to exchange gifts?*

3. Jesus, just look at #2.
4. We've already broken up three times.
5. Although she threw out us "trying to be together, again," I did not commit to it.
6. Bonus: The reason I didn't see her last Christmas is because I fled our toxic codependence. She can be enchanting and infuriating and an emotional terrorist. I'm even worse. Chatting with her can pluck at my heartstrings, even two oceans away.

Clearly number six is the only real reason. Plus, I want to not feel bad when I meet Naomi Watt's sister at the bar tonight. Suzanne and Naomi actually don't look that dissimilar. Hmmm.

•

"Georgie, you ready? I booked an Ubah. Should be here in seven minutes."

"Yeah, I'm ready. Be right down." I tug the straps of the Baby Bjorn. I've tucked in a few treats in between the magazines. Gum, a Ziploc of cashews and a spare t-shirt. If I'm gonna wear a reversed backpack all night, I'm gonna use it. I found a few flashlights in the garage and was tempted to pack one, but my penchant for over-preparedness can be a bit much.

Suzanne is looking at her own reflection in the sliding glass door, pretty pleased with herself.

"Jesus fucking Christ."

"Too subtle? Hee hee."

She's wearing fishnets, leather shorts and a teeny apron, where the

Edible Complex is affixed.

"Betty Crocker porn? Thank god I don't have a sweet tooth. Especially as you keep making the Blue Steel face in your reflection. Where did you get that string to keep the monster cookie in place?"

"At the butchah shop."

"Smart. You look unbelievable. Let's go, mommy. I can see the cab's headlights through the fence."

•

The Uber driver is in no rush, which I like, as neither are we. It's nice to have a little one-on-one time with Suzanne, enjoying our neurotic arranged marriage.

She lets a lazy right turn slide her body across the seat, smashing against me, and doesn't bother to move back.

We pass Ravesis—the most sporty bar in Bondi. American expats love it, due to all of the TVs. Bars are for drinking, solving unsolvable problems and falling in love. Therefore, I'm not a huge fan of TV's in bars. But I've never been a sports fan. I know I'm alone on this one, as the place is packed. Craigo loves his sport, but he prefers spectating from his mancave—even though Ravesis is across the street from We've Gotchya Back. I might be the only American he can tolerate. Hopefully that sticks.

I see Philip.

Prince Charming is sucking on his cig-nature electronic device, with some other mean-drunk clientele.

"Hey, isn't that Philip Morris?"

"Yeah, he looks upside down. Must've been on the piss all day, watching footie."

And here comes his designated driver.

Veronica pulls to a stop, immediately adjacent to our stealth cab. She smiles at Philip, and he gives her the *Stop. Wait.* power-hand gesture that you'd give a disobedient dog.

"Can't believe the poor thing is wearing a turtleneck. Must be thirty degrees outside."

"I can't convert to Fahrenheit that fast, but it's gotta be at least eighty-five. You're right. It's odd."

"Wait. Is Charlotte with her?"

Veronica turns to the back seat and attends to Charlotte. I'm closer and get a full view of her. The seatbelt catches her turtleneck, revealing a bruise where a hickey might be. If you gave hickeys with your thumb.

"Oh dear."

"Mother…fucker." It's only for a second, but we both see it. And she didn't get it from hanging laundry.

"I can't believe he's having Veronica come pick him up."

"The wank."

"Excuse me? Mr. Driver?"

"What can I do fah you, mate?"

"Can you stop here for one minute? My goddaughter's right there. Want to say a quick hello."

"A quick one, ay? Bit hectic down here."

"Thanks!"

"Georgie, whattaya …" But I'm already struggling to get out of the cab, and the Baby Bjorn is hardly a tracksuit.

"Philip! Hey!"

Too drunk to notice me, Philip opens the door to the passenger side.

I wanted to talk to him alone. He probably would have hit me. But I don't care.

*Tap. Tap. Tap.*

Veronica rolls down the window.

"George! Hello! Yah're out late!"

"Captain Bloody America!"

"Yeah, uh…we're going to Ava's show." I point to my absurd costume, "Fancy dress."

"Absent Fathah?"

"Dang. That's pretty good. No, it's…" I'm drowning. "I saw Charlotte…wanted to…"

I glance at Charlotte. I caught it at the wake, but it didn't hit me. PJ's eyes. They're an exact duplicate. Even dozing, I recognize them underneath her fluttering eyelids. She looks like PJ going back to bed after a two-day bender. Not a care in the world.

Veronica takes a breath to speak. But Philip Morris cuts her off.

"Anothah time. Visiting hours are ovah, mate." He turns his glare to Veronica, and she knows not to disobey.

She starts rolling up the window, before her salutation.

"A bit late for Char, George. We've gotta ruuu…" Veronica takes her foot off the brake, severing our conversation. Philip Morris has already disengaged, fiddling with the radio. Dickhead. How does he not have *Triple J* as a preset? Even I know that.

Defeated, I walk back to the Uber.

Only two minutes have passed, but it feels like a lifetime. Opening the door, I see Suzanne handing our driver a twenty, and I want to marry her.

"No worries, doll. I'm a godfathah mahself." He gracefully declines.

"Goddaughters always need earrings. Thank you fah yah patience." She drops the twenty in the front passenger seat.

I give a small, appreciative smile.

"Suzanne, you're a queen."

"'Course. How's the godfathah?" She teases.

"Fuck Suzanne. I just…I just wanted to…"

"I know, love. I know."

•

She sends a text to Craigo. I can see his shaved head in the crowd, in line for the show. He's got a noose around his neck, and it's choking a box of Home Brand Cocoa Puffs—the local generic brand.

I pop out of the Uber and help Suzanne. Her outfit could fail at any moment.

"Cereal Killer, really? I thought I had the laziest possible costume."

"Aw, mate. I had a tricked out kit, with a full Deadpool suit, but Hannah puked all ovah it. I had to get her cleaned up before dropping her at her mum's, and this was all I had time fah." He looks at my rig. "And what are you? Futah Stepfathah?"

"Damn. Everyone's got me beat tonight. No." I pull out a magazine, and the Ziploc of cashews hits the ground. "See?" I point to the Bjorn, then to the magazines. "Daddy Issues."

"Pretty dark. But I like where yah head's at. And Suzie, look at you. What is that? A chocolate dunny? She bangs like the dunny door in a storm?"

Brothers are mean. Dunny = an Australian outhouse. *She bangs like the dunny door in a storm* is the equivalent of saying she fucks like a banshee. Classy, Craigo.

"Arsehole! And quit calling me that! My name is Suzanne! I'm not an energy drink!"

"Hey man, that's not nice. She's Edible Complex. It's actually pretty good."

"My apologies Suzaaanne. It was either that or Mothah Teresa. Complete toss up."

He giggles. She punches him.

He checks his phone.

"Ah, let's go. She's got us on the list."

We walk into the Beach Road Hotel. It's more road than beach. It's a misnomer, like how Manhattan Beach does not resemble Manhattan in any way. It's grittier than Bondi Beach. And there isn't a single tourist. Besides me.

"Ava's in the back, warming up. Gets a bit of stage fright. Let's grab a beer."

We navigate to the bar.

"Shall we steal this, draw a cocktail glass with a phallic stick and olive under it, and print five hundred?" It's the title of their drink menu: *Fancy a Stiff One?*

"Already been done." He catches the bartender's attention. "Four Coopahs? Appreciate it."

"Hey, grab Suzanne a vodka cran?"

"You've gotta be quickah than that. Her outfit's a hit."

True.

Three dudes hover around her. She's already been handed a glass of wine. A pang of jealousy hits, but I table it.

"Hey, listen to how fucked up this is. Philip Morris?"

"Yeah?" He sips his beer but locks eyes with me.

"We just saw him outside Ravesis. Veronica was picking him up."

His eyes flare.

"At ten o'clock at night? She's gotta newborn at home!"

"It gets worse. Charlotte was in the car. And Veronica was wearing a turtleneck, hiding a bruise." I pantomime grabbing his throat.

"That fuckwit."

We take a few sips and stand in silence. The bar continues to fill, with the increasing sound moving into the empty spaces.

"I feel like I've created a situation with a self-fulfilling prophecy."

"Ah, don't start with that noise again."

"No, no. It's not the guilt talking. It's like I jinxed it. I was so devastated when PJ died. I felt like I was running back home to LA. To get away from it. To lick my wounds and put it behind me."

"Yeah?"

"But when I heard about Charlotte, it gave me a sense of purpose. 'I'm gonna go check on her'—like I'm Jack fucking Ryan. And I come here for closure. And now it's become funeral tourism, as you and

Suzanne do everything you can to welcome me here. And meeting you guys has given me closure. I hope I've done that for you, too, in some way, having spent every waking moment with PJ this last year."

I'm starting to spiral, and Craigo intercepts. He takes my empty pint glass to replace it with a fresh beer.

I open my hand for it, but he pulls a jujitsu twist, grabs my wrist and exposes my scars.

"Georgie. The weird Israeli guy, Tisk Task."

"Tsvika."

"Whatevah. Taskah told me. I read the autopsy. The reports. Even using Google Translate from Spanish, you get the gist." He turns my palm over. "Just look at yah hands."

We both look at my bullet wound. At the remnants of the cuts on my hands—from grabbing the dock posts covered in barnacles. The scars born from hours of stitches. From trying to save PJ.

I've got nothing.

"You wanna talk about a self-fulfilling prophecy? When our parents died? True irony, my dad, a panel beatah, dies in a car crash…" Panel beater = an auto body shop owner/worker.

"I know. That's awful. I'm so sorry."

"Nah, it's been ages. Thanks. Anyway, PJ? He shows up late to the funeral. Late to his own parents' funeral. Why? He got into a scrap with some guys ovah a few dollahs worth of weed. He thought the bag was a little light, so he chimes off—taking the piss outah the dealer. This isn't the States. Where everything is legalized and they sell cocaine from parking metahs. Drugs have to come a looong way to get here. And they're expensive. You do not want to question these guys."

My eyes well up.

"PJ is not one to tolerate injustice, especially when it comes to partying." The second beer has hit, and I'm getting too emotional to change my verbs back to past tense. Goddamn, I miss him.

"So PJ, he shows up next to the casket. He's got a bloody lip and underneath his suit? He's hiding two broken ribs that we won't uncovah fah weeks. You don't tell a Russian streetsman his forty dollah bag of green looks like it's worth thirty. Not if you wanna keep all yah teeth."

"I'm sorry. But I think that story is fantastic."

He nods, takes a sip and barks back at me.

"That's not the point, mate."

"OK?"

"The point is, while we were waiting at the church, Suzanne and I made a dark joke—that the next family event would eithah be PJ's shotgun wedding or his funeral."

"Whoa. Fuuuck. That is dark."

"Cheeky bastard. He went out with a bang, didn't he? Knocked 'em both out."

"Self-fulfilling prophecy."

*I called it.* Not me, Craigo. It's a shirt they have printed at the shop, and it might be my favorite. But pointing it out right now feels ungracious. The best jokes are always better left unsaid.

"Craigo, you're a knight among men."

The bartender has refueled us, and Craigo toasts me with the first sip of his third.

My hand has been resting in the Bjorn this whole time, like the warm front pocket of a hoodie. Maybe being a dad wouldn't be so arduous and uncomfortable after all.

We down our beers and scan the floor for Suzanne. Spotted. She's making her way toward us, holding another drink that she got for free. I sneak in one last comment, as she snakes through the packed crowd.

"But what do we do about Philip Morris? We can't have Charlotte living with a…"

He cuts me off.

"That wank? It's simple. We sit him down for a chat. I don't know what we can do criminally, but one thing's fah sure—he's not gonna be living undah the same roof as my niece, if he's put hands on Vee."

"But what if that doesn't work?"

"Plan B. Thought that was yah depahtment."

•

Thank god I'm not a woman. Suzanne is absolutely destroyed. I'm not alone in noticing. Craigo is well on his way, but he's unstoppable. He pulls her out the pack of hungry males circling her vulnerability. I help, but it doesn't hold a candle to Craigo's decisiveness.

A few minutes later in the cab, Suzanne dozes on my shoulder.

"Two stops, mate. Just a bit up Blair Street, then take these two."

The cabbie is nonplussed by the train wreck that just dropped into his backseat. Craigo turns to me.

"Make sure she's sorted? She tied one on a bit."

"Will do. And tell Ava thanks and that she was great. Pretty cool of her to step in and do backup vocals for the headliner. I'd like to have seen the full set."

"Indeed. Sadly, I won't see her aftah. I've gotta grab Hannah early. She knows the single dad drill."

Is Suzanne drooling on my shoulder?

"With all due respect, Ava was looking pretty fine up there. Her vocal range is unbelievable."

"I saw you gawking at her tits, mothahfuckah!"

"No I was not. OK. Maybe twice."

"So was I! And every othah bloke in the bar! But I'm the only one that gets to unwrap the present undah the tree."

"And you're the man for the job, Craigo. Great night."

"You sorted on cash?" He looks at the meter.

"Yeah, my turn anyway—you bought the drinks. Say hi to Hannah for me."

"Right. Catch you in the pm."

I give the cabbie our address, and we're off. Suzanne waits five seconds, turns herself into a grocery bag and crawls into my arms. She rests her lips on my neck. Not kissing me. But not not kissing me.

•

Fishing the back door key out of my pocket, Suzanne startles.

"What's hiding in there, love?"

"Just trying to get us inside."

I'm carrying 80% of her body weight.

"Thank you, Geooorgiiieee."

It sounds cute, but her talking requires her to stop kissing, errr, not

not kissing my neck.

"I didn't save you from that wolf pack. Craigo did."

"Not from the boys. Saving me from mahself."

"Possibly true." The back door slides open easily. "Come on. Let's go upstairs."

"Yes!"

She goes from standing (leaning) to kicking both of her legs up, diagonal across my torso. She wants me to carry her. I close the back door behind us and head up the stairs.

I can carry her, but I make a note to do more squats. Swimmer's bodies are so top heavy.

Much to her chagrin, I pass both of our bedrooms and set her on the top of the toilet seat in my bathroom.

Because my bathroom has a tub.

"You're covered in cookie crumbs, and the makeup smudges make you look like an edible zombie."

"Edible Mumbie!"

I laugh.

"Something. OK. Rinse off. Even if you have to lie down. I'll grab your bathrobe."

She drops her clothes on the tile, like they were an afterthought. Drunk adults and all children love the bathtub.

Her half-bath half-shower is brief.

I set her towel and bathrobe on the sink and avert my eyes.

I walk outside the bathroom and stand by the door.

"I can dry mahself! I'm not a child!"

It's unclear who this statement is directed to.

I hear her abrasively drying off. Then, she sprints by me to her room. She leaves the towel and robe in her wake. I grab them and wipe up the trail of water. She's currently a strong candidate for alcohol poisoning.

I check on her.

Sheet at waist, pillows on floor, she's got her arms thrown above her head. She's so exposed; I hope I'm deserving of this level of trust.

I pull a sheet up over her.

"Are you mad?"

"No, of course not."

She flops around on the bed. Trying to get comfortable. Soaking everything. She lands on her side, facing me, and pats the bed. Her torso is uncovered, and she's unabashed.

"Sit with me, Georgie." I tell myself that if she pukes, chokes on it and dies, that's on me. "Unless yah're mad?"

"Why would I be mad? Because you're drunk? Absolutely not. You deserve to let off some steam. Plus, I've drank with you almost half a dozen times now, and you always maintain control."

"Right?!"

I'm sitting upright, not getting into bed. She curls into the nook I've created.

"You don't know what it's like to be a girl. You always have to keep it togethah. I just wanted to play and not worry. For once. And knowing I had two bodyguards? Made it easy. It was nice."

"I can imagine. Craigo creates a safe, welcoming environment wherever he goes. No harm no foul."

"You too, love."

"Thank you? Sorry, taking compliments is hard. What'd you think of the show? Pretty good, right?"

"She was aaawesome." She shifts and rests her head on my thigh. "Georgie, put some music on, and get undah the covers…"

Thirty seconds of silence and she's gone. It's not a snore so much as a drawl. As if her sleep has an Appalachian accent.

Sometimes, blacking out is our friend.

If Suzanne had a band, they'd be named…

Miss Chievous.

# 6

4am.

Suzanne is breathing normally. No risk of her choking on her own vomit like Jimi Hendrix. Or, as we're in Australia, Bon Scott.

I want my own bed. And sleep. But I only find one.

The goddamn birds. You can't hear them in Suzanne's room.

Yet another benefit.

A restless hour.

5am.

A quick check of the Bondi Icebergs website—the pool opens in an hour. If I make coffee slow enough, plus the walk over the hill, I should arrive just as they're opening up.

*Suzanne—*

*Went for a swim at Icebergs.*

*Will return with coffee around 8.*

*Sleep tight.*

*Georgie*

Suzanne has a fancy espresso machine, and I'd kill for a quad espresso, but it's too loud. The electric kettle does the trick, and the French press makes me miss making coffee this way. More satisfying. Like everything else in life. When you actually earn it.

It's a quiet twenty-minute walk over the hill.

"G'day! Early start?"

"Yeah, couldn't sleep. Only one solution." The trim waist and over-tan face of the attendant says it all—lifelong swimmer.

"Good man. Well you've got it all to yahself! At least fah a bit."

"Yeah, a bit groggy from the Coopers last night. But glad I rallied."

"Nice one. You a membah?"

"No, I just wanna pay the guest fee."

"Five and a half, then. First time to Sydney?"

"Yep, thanks so much."

Here we go again. I have exact change. I take a few steps to avoid hearing: *Canadian*?

It is the most stunning pool I've ever seen in my life. A full fifty meters, with waves crashing on the outer wall and a restaurant above to spectate.

I could stay here forever.

•

Most lap pools are twenty-five meters. About two or three times the length of a suburban backyard pool. University and Olympic events are held in fifty-meter pools. Even though it's twice the distance, it feels like four times.

Some say that swimming is a thinking person's sport. Others say it's a dull person's sport. All of that time, repeating the same stroke, with nothing to do. Either it's meditative or agonizingly boring.

Both are true. But even in a small pool, you have less time to think than you'd expect. Because swimming takes thought. Did I take thirteen strokes to get across or fourteen? How's my breathing? Keep head down. Focus on the hips and the back—save the shoulders—there's a long way to go.

The meditative part is quite short. A few seconds of clarity is always followed by a self-correction, before hitting the wall. The wall is the reset button. After pushing off, you have almost no recall of what important problem was being solved twelve feet ago.

But not in the fifty meter.

A fifty takes about forty-five seconds to get across. With your head down in the pool, that's a long time. It is enough time to have a thought, reflect on it, chew on it a bit and come to a conclusion. You might even get it back, once you hit the wall.

•

Toward the end of my set, the hardcore locals arrive. Unheated ocean water every day at 6:55am? Impressive. A late 30's jokester with a belly and excess confidence reminds me of Craigo.

I'm envious of Craigo. He's unflappable. He's pure. Violence against women + little niece = bad. Confrontation = solution.

Don't overthink it.

•

7:45am.

Dead silence.

I tiptoe upstairs with our drinks.

Even face down and hung-over, she looks stunning. A sliver of the sheet covers her backside.

Suzanne gets her share of attention. But more and more, it's her inner beauty that draws me to her. She is so inherently kind and thoughtful. That and her brutal honesty. I still find myself curious about her. I continue to sneak glances at her, just like I did at the airport.

The smell of the coffee wakes her.

"Yah're up early."

"Swam at Icebergs. That place is so beautiful, it looks filtered."

"Pretty nice spot, ay?"

I'm nervous to touch her. We've not yet been in this kind of proximity completely sober.

I tug the sheet up over her shoulders, as she rolls onto her side to grab the piccolo.

"Mmm." She takes a sip.

"I'm gonna go take a shower."

"Stay for a minute?" She rubs my thigh, sealing the invitation.

"Just to get the salt water and sweat off from the walk. But I can come back? If you want?"

"Please."

She tugs at my shirt. I don't resist. A long lingering kiss.

The sheet falls off her shoulders, and she leaves it down at her tummy.

I stroke her neck. I every-so-lightly pull one of her shoulders back, and she follows, exposing her chest to me. Another invitation.

I lick her nipple, then drag it lightly against my two front teeth with my tongue.

She gasps.

"OK. Be right back."

Her eyes dart open, as I stand for the door.

"Georgie! Not fair."

"Two words. Edible Complex."

"Aggghhh."

She sighs and dissolves into bed. I hit the shower.

Does your penis ever get cleaner than when it is three quarters erect in the shower?

Nope.

The speed in which I dry off? Superhuman.

The eight seconds it takes to walk from my bathroom to her door feels like a month.

"Hey."

"Well, hello." She perks up and looks at me. "Yah're naked!"

"I have a towel on?"

"Come here, American boy."

We kiss for ages. So long, I wish I'd worn lip balm.

I'm on the fence as to whether we should take it further.

Suzanne decides, by yanking my towel off and dropping it on the floor.

I pull her on top of me. I lift her up, pull her legs over my shoulders and consume her lady parts.

"Ahhh. Am I suffocating you?"

"Nah, uh." (a muffled version of no).

She fidgets.

"Are you sure this is comfortable?" I stop and look up at her.

"It's perfect. Feel." I pull her hand around to my cock. "I think I might come before you."

"That would be so hot!"

I grip myself and link the rhythm of each stroke to devouring her. I can taste her, and see her, and…it doesn't take long. I hit her lower back with my man-juice. She fully lets go.

Towel. Wipe. Nap.

I doze to the sound of her writing a text.

•

*@200dollarhoodie when is it ok to check your phone, after sex?*

*@AskEsquire 1. Never or 2. ten seconds after she does or 3. while she's in the bathroom.*

The *Esquire* portal has a search feature, and it comes in handy. While Suzanne was in the bathroom, I used the bathroom in the hallway, next to my room. She really needs to turn the sound off her phone, because, even while peeing, I could hear her texting away. I found @200dollarhoodie's post faster than you can say *keyword* and dropped my response into the queue. Sometimes working in social media is dreamy. The ease of communicating offsets the pain of the actual content.

I look at my Speedo. Still soaking wet. It's not drying in the bathroom. I grab it and bring it into my small room—a study really—and lay it out in front of the desk fan. No dice.

A thought. I grab my earphones, yank the cord out, test it and then create a clothesline across the window. Victory. The wind makes it flutter a tad. It looks drier already.

Very pleased with my own ingenuity, I head back to my, uh, *roommate*?

"You know you can use the bathroom in here, love."

"I didn't want to interrupt your real-time text conversation."

"What?" But it's not a question.

"It's OK. Is it Lance?"

She sighs.

"Yes."

"Hmmm."

"I'm sorry."

"It's OK."

"Does it make you sad?"

"I don't know. I'd say it hurts my feelings, but it doesn't, really. Just jealous. And I'm hardly in a position to judge."

"We just have a connection."

"I know. You spent the night with him the night of your brother's funeral, the next day welcoming his fiancé. That's more than a connection. I know I sound like a judgy prick. But it made total sense to me."

"You do sound like a judgy prick. He's a small weakness. That happens to be very convenient."

"I know the feeling."

"Plus, no one is 100% single, you know? Everyone has someone on the back burnah. It's too lonely to be alive without a pilot light on. Look at you, with yah bird back home."

"Shawna? Yeeeah. Can we maybe not talk about her? While we're in bed together?"

"'Course, love."

I wish I could have the computer in bed with me, as something about Suzanne sparks solid love advice:

*@AskEsquire When your new crush asks about an old girlfriend, touch her. The contact will keep her from questioning your allegiance.*

I nestle back into Suzanne, reach down and stroke her leg.

Sometimes, I take my own love advice.

Sometimes.

"Want to hear something a wee bit malicious? About Lance?"

"Always."

"I make him use a condom. I say it's because he's got a fiancé. But the condoms? They give him anxiety. He can only maintain an erection every third try. So, he prays that the third time's the charm, and I occasionally don't have to sleep alone. Is that so bad? There are some nights I just can't bear it."

"Ruthless. Understandable. Endorsed."

She straddles me.

"Correct answah. Why dontchya check to see if my IUD is still in place?"

•

Hours later, sleepwalking from jetlag, I search my *Esquire* portal for IUD, hoping to define it as: *dead baby catch 'n' release.* But I'm already caught up on work. And I know my cringe-worthy IUD metaphor stems from the anxiety of not knowing what to do about Philip Morris.

I close my computer and head back to Suzanne's room.

•

From a deep slumber, I hear the downstairs sliding glass door open.

"Wakey wakey!"

Uh oh.

Craigo is here.

Suzanne and I saucer-eye each other, and I exit the bed quietly.

We both fear getting caught. At least getting caught this way. I tiptoe-sprint back to my room. At least he won't hear my voice coming from Suzanne's room. I yell.

"Craigo! Be right down! Slept in."

When your sister lives in your parents' old house, you treat it as comfortably as your own. I can hear Craigo firing up the electric teapot and rummaging through the fridge.

"G'day!"

"Hey. I fell back asleep. Hit Icebergs early and…"

"The jetlag, it'll hit and then just smash you back!" The definition of a good friend is someone who makes excuses for you. His familiar movements in the kitchen calm me.

"Yeah, big night. Couldn't sleep. Crushed a few coffees before swimming, then tinkered with work. Ended up passing back out. What time is it?"

"11am. You've not been here a week, yet. You've got an excuse. Plus you were clearly the soberest of us all, so…well hello, sunshine!" Suzanne skulks down the stairs.

"Mornin' Craigo. One of those toasties better be fah me."

Wow. Her game is tight. And her robe better be super tight, as I'm confident that some of my DNA remains underneath.

I bury my head in the fridge. Gonna let Suzanne handle this one.

"Feelin' a bit average?"

"Not too too bad. I should've eaten something last night."

"Didn't you have a bite of cookie for an appetizer and Georgie for the main course, Suze?"

"Well, you both are always so busy rooting each othah at the shop, having a shag ovah the silkscreenah, I had to at least get a nibble."

"There she is!"

Sibling combative homeostasis restored.

Craigo lays out toast, and I grab the almond butter that I've been eyeing for a few days. He pops another round into the toaster. Good man. He turns toward me.

"You sorted to have a bit of a chat with Veronica? The man-twat is off at training. We can have her to ourselves."

"Poor thing. Buttah wouldn't melt in her mouth."

"Huh?"

She's spreading butter on toast. This idiom goes over my head.

"She's a good girl. Wholesome. Wouldn't hurt a fly. Buttah wouldn't melt in her mouth."

"Ah, got it. I like that one."

"Let's head to the shop, do a couple of errands, then kill two birds with one stone—start up the Moke and take her out to Vee's."

"Yes!"

"Wanna join, Suze?"

"Craigo, she's gonna kill you, if you keep calling her that." This is my version of fighting for her honor.

"Suzaaanne?"

"Naaah…I'll hold down the fort and cure my hangovah with the television."

"Suit yahself."

"Is there time to make Charlotte a present at the shop? I came up with some kids t-shirt ideas. They're not as dark as the rest."

"Whattaya got?"

"One is a bunch of bassinettes, full of babies wearing camo onesies. Simply: *Infantry.*"

"Ha, that's cute."

"All you Yanks are such war mongahs. And I've already gotchya beat." He pulls out his phone and shows me a pastel onesie—it's got a spiderweb, with Charlotte spelled out.

"*Charlotte's Web.* Untoppable. Maybe I could at least get her the book, to go with it?"

"Sure thing. Eat up. The Moke'll take a bit to get up and running."

"What were the dark ones?" Suzanne asks. An unfounded phenomenon is curiosity of the other partner after sex. On an interesting scale of 1-10, I am a 2. Now that I've kissed Suzanne, I'm a 5. I don't want to disappoint her. Not because of our physical intimacy but because I care. It makes me reluctant to share my throwaway, thoughtless quips.

"Let's see. One is a card. The front is a picture of a cactus shaped like a heart. The inside reads: *Love is like a Succulent. It Thrives in Neglect.*"

"Oh dear."

"Brilliant."

"I was also thinking of a maternity shirt, and over the belly it says: *Plan C.*"

"Ugh…Georgiiiie."

"OK. Skip that one. What about a onesie for baby girls? Kinda on the theme of yah girl's band, Craigo: *Miss Take.*" They shake their heads. "It's got a double meaning…"

"We get it, mate. These are terrible. Yah first few were a'right, but these last ones aren't exactly a celebration of the miracle of life, ay?"

"Seven billion miracles are enough?"

"Dontchya teach bloody swimming to kids?"

"I write a love advice column. And most of the submissions are from people so incompetent, they shouldn't be procreating. I strongly include myself in this generalization." I look at Suzanne. She feigns a smile.

•

"Help me get her outside, ay? We've gotta start her out in the open air."

We roll the buggy out the front doors. It feels illegal. The Moke is absolutely tiny. It's a good thing Suzanne didn't want to come. She'd have to sit on my lap.

Hmmm.

We push.

"Christ that bloody hurts."

"Really? What does this thing weigh? Twelve hundred pounds? It's already rolling."

"My head, mate. Ava gave me a bit of a booty call. We finished a bottle of wine and then we groped each othah for an hour. Fun but, not sure if I remember all of it."

"Yeah, drunk sex is kinda like eating a sandwich with a spoon. Ineffective. Messy."

"Nah, more like eating a sundae without one. Messy. Delicious."

"You're on fire today, Craigo."

"A'right. You wanna pop 'round to Gertrude & Alice's, to see if they've got *Charlotte's Web*? I need to prime her up a bit. It'll take about twenty minutes."

"Yeah, but the bookstore will only take five. Do you guys have cheap international phone service?"

"'Course. Gotta call mainland China twice a week, at least. Need to call yah mum?"

"Uh, yeah. Just a quick touch base."

Who I really want is to call Tsvika. To see if he can do anything about Philip Morris. I'm not sure what he can do, but he's the most resourceful person I know. Plus, he's a gun owner.

Withholding this from Craigo feels wrong, but it's the right call.

"It barely costs a cent. Go crazy."

•

International, country code, area code, number. I've never successfully dialed overseas on the first try in my life.

Fifteen rings. Tsvika is some sort of government agent. I can almost hear the call being redirected and tracked.

"Alo?" He either says a contracted *Hello* or an inaudible *Shalom*. No matter.

"Tsviks. It's George."

"Ah, George. Yes."

"All good in Panama?"

"Yes." Tsvika is not one for small talk. "PJ family? Is OK?"

"Yeah, we've had all the services. And folks are moving on. He was pretty heavily loved here."

"Yes. PJ many friends."

"So true. A succinct synopsis, Tsviks."

"Eh?"

"It was a compliment. Never mind. Hey, so can you look into a guy for me? His name is Philip Mo… errr, Philip LeCompte. He's a cop here."

"The policeman? Yes. I have spoken. His attorney."

"Yeah, yeah. The estate stuff again?"

"Yes."

"Prick."

"Not good person. Agreed."

"But PJ had nothing. Nothing."

"No. Not nothing. The school. Hotel. His share of land."

"But that's all your money."

"Eh…no. My father, some. But Israel pay. PJ is bounty. You too, George. Is small, but…"

"The reward. I don't want any of it."

"Is fine, George. I give to PJ. But portion of PJ's estate go to heirs. His daughter. The parents control."

"And Philip wants to know what his potential cut is?"

"Yes."

"That. Makes. Me. Fucking. Sick."

"Unfortunate, yes."

"Ugh."

"George. Apologies. Nothing I can…"

"It's OK. I appreciate you realizing PJ's dream. It's still something. A lot. And Tsviks?"

"Yes?

"Philip. He is a bad, bad guy."

"A criminal?"

"Well, yes, actually. He is a criminal. I'm highly confident he beats his girlfriend."

"Terrible."

"Can you guys, you know…do something?"

"Heh. George. The men who hurts the women? Agree. Should be punished. I? I cannot. We cannot. Even if he is criminal. Unless…"

"Unless what?"

"Unless he is war criminal."

"Oh."

"George, I want the helping. Of course."

"I know, Tsviks. I know."

# 7

"What's the plan?"

"Bit nervous, Georgie? This isn't a black ops mission. We're not SAS Commandos. We're gonna stop by, give little Char a squeeze and have a bit of a chat with Vee."

"Yeah, OK. I dunno. I'm nervous."

"We're just popping by to see my niece. Remembah, Vee used to work fah me. No worries."

He's right. But this was 100% the purpose of my trip. Other than getting wasted every day and developing a little more than a thing for PJ's sister. Jesus. Now, I'm taking a book to his love child.

•

"Hello there."

"Hiya Craigo! Nice to see you. Hello George!" We double cheek kiss, etc. "Little Charlotte is having a kip but should be up shortly."

Craigo gives her a cheek kiss and a bonus squeeze. She flinches involuntarily and gasps. This tells me two things. 1. Her gasp is not excitement; it's pain. This is the textbook reaction when hugging someone with bruised or broken ribs (yes, I am CPR certified). 2. While trying to unwind herself from Craigo, her shawl falls to the ground. It's easily ninety degrees. She ain't cold. Her arms are covered in bruises. Covered.

Whoa.

We brush past it (at least on the surface) and hand over the gifts.

She's grateful. But mostly to have more surface area to cover the evidence of her abuse—especially the big picture book of *Charlotte's Web.*

"Aren't you both so sweet. Let me go set these down. Please forgive me; I'm having a lactating moment and need to change my shirt."

I did not witness evidence of this. Nor did Craigo. He gives me the *that's bullshit* eyebrow furrow. I whisper, as she exits.

"Did you see her arms?"

"I did. Someone should assassinate that fuckwit."

"Now that we have near irrefutable proof that Philip is violent, I'm even more on board with him not returning here. Certainly not if Charlotte is here."

"Mate, that's not fucking happening."

"Can we at least try to get Veronica there slowly? Ease her into it?"

"Why?"

"We're about to blow up her life. The least we can do is act like she had some part of it. Some input."

"She's the one that chose that fuckwit."

"She's been beaten up enough. We've got to protect her, too."

He chews on it.

"A'right. A'right. Yah're right. She's the mothah of my niece and always will be. Got a bit laser focused on Char."

"Of course. Regardless, we need Vee as an ally, whatever the outcome."

"Agreed."

We stare at each other for a second. Take a breath.

I look around, fixated on how bizarre this scenario is.

"I can't believe we're on a social call at PJ's baby mama's house. Feels so surreal."

"Speak fah yahself. I can't believe this is the only one."

"Be nice."

When we were roommates in Panama, PJ bought countless condoms from the local bodega. He was a man-whore. But he was pretty responsible. At least from what I saw. Maybe he wasn't so cautious when he was here. We'll never know.

She returns.

In long sleeves.

The small fan she flicks on in the kitchen doesn't dent the stale air.

I wanna take my pants off. And not because I'm thinking about Suzanne.

"Char's still dead asleep. Either of you care for a spot of tea?"

"Bottle of piss would be heavenly."

I shake my head. It's noon. A beer does sound tempting. But it's clear she's making some herbal concoction for herself.

"I'd love some tea. Would it be OK if I throw a few ice cubes in it?"

"Of course. It's nice to not be the only one drinking tea. Think I'll do the same."

I smirk at Craigo, making sure he noted the points I just scored.

Those plug-in teapots are awesome.

She brings our drinks out. The ice in my iced (hot) tea melts, as she walks from the kitchen to the living room.

"Cheers, Vee."

Craigo takes down half of his beer.

Looks delicious.

And cold.

I sip my lukewarm tea.

"Thank you. Perfect."

You know when it's Halloween, and every female is dressed like Sexy Snow White, but one resists and wears something conservative? The smart one that opts for some version of the Petty Coat Revolution? But she doesn't own it? And ends up standing in the corner looking uncomfortable all night? That's Veronica in long sleeves, as we sit here in t-shirts.

Craigo finishes his beer before Veronica has taken her first sip. His wherewithal is not to be denied. He just drove a fifty-year-old car here and acts like he owns the place. How long until he pulls his second beer from the fridge without asking?

"You all sorted, love?"

"Of course. Everything is great."

"You sure?"

"Yeah. All good."

He motions me to be good cop. In Craigo's mind, good cop is a just a synonym for soft. For me, the role is not a stretch.

"I think what Craigo means is do you need any help? I know I'll only be here for a few more days, but I'd be happy to…"

"Nah, nah. I'm great."

"You sure?" Craigo is on his feet. He carries his empty bottle into the kitchen. He opens the fridge without asking and pops another. He's a machine. I will say, they are well stocked—with the bottom half of the fridge dedicated to a case of Victoria Bitter.

"Yeah, 'course. You guys have been fantastic. The money. The offahs for help. It's been wondahful. You don't have to do anything more."

"But yah're family, Vee." Craigo stays standing. Assuming a position of power. Plus, he'll want to be near the fridge for number three. I sip my tea, watching the last ice cube liquify. "We got sent a few papahs on PJ's 'estate'." Craigo takes a long pull and postures. "Whattah laugh that is—the guy owning two pairs of boardies to his name."

This is untrue. His estate includes a modest piece of land in Panama, courtesy of the Israeli government. What I don't know is if it includes some portion of a defunct t-shirt shop and the million dollar house I slept in last night. I'm dying to know. But it's not my place to ask.

Veronica looks embarrassed and fidgets.

"Yeah, well, it was Philip's idea. I do think he's right, though." She looks at us for approval. "He's been talking of adopting Charlotte. Wants to make sure…"

"But Vee, come on. The prenatal support classes? The Rolls-Royce of strollahs? You know we've got you sorted."

This? I did not know.

"Yeah, 'course. Craigo, you've been amazing. Ahhhmazing. He just wants to know what he's getting into."

"Why does it mattah? Why all this attorney back 'n' forth? You know we've gotchya back."

Redundant?

Craigo slow-walking her into the Philip ultimatum is impressive. A rare glimpse of his patience.

"Uhh, yeah…no…you do…"

I'm gonna feel pathetic, if I don't say something.

"How does Philip treat you?"

"He's nice. Good."

Bullshit.

"Suzanne. You…" Craigo rolls his eyes at my misstep. "Sorry, Veronica. The jetlag still has me. Sorry. But are you cool? With Philip? He seems a bit…I dunno…domin…"

"Domineering."

Craigo has stopped looking like he's seeking his next beer and is fully engaged. He's present. Which is more than I can say for myself.

I'm always thinking two steps forward and four steps back. Never living in the now.

"Exactly. Domineering. Is Philip who you want as a partner? What about Charlotte?"

She mulls it over for a second. It feels like an eternity. There are scattered pictures of them throughout the family room. A lot of beach shots. One of Philip and what looks like his father (older, same haircut) fishing at another picture-perfect Australian beach.

Looking at the photos, he doesn't really smile; he smirks with his nostrils flared. Slack jawed, every single picture has him looking like he's about to inhale a garbanzo bean through his nose. Creepy nostril flarer.

"Philip's really good to me. Helps me look aftah Char." Define: *Good to me*—but I keep it to myself. "There wasn't exactly a line of admirers, when I was up the duff, you know." Up the duff = pregnant. It makes knocked up sound classy.

"Vee, yah're covahed in bruises. I can still see the outline of where Prince Charming…

"Ah, nooo, I hit the cupboard…"

"Love, I've been hit by cupboards, and I've been hit by fists. You didn't get that grabbin' fah a tin of biscuits." Craigo knows what he's talking about. He was a legit boxer in high school. I came across a few of his trophies, when I was scavenging the garage for my Daddy Issues ensemble.

She sighs, defeated. Some stirring from the baby monitor and it recalibrates us.

"Veronica, we didn't come here to judge you. We're concerned. PJ was the best friend I've ever had. Ever. And to think of his daughter living in the same house as a guy who's got a violent temper, well, it…"

Craigo's face gives my speech a C minus.

"Vee. We actually are here to tell you what to do. If that wank lays a finger on my niece, evah, I will fucking execute him."

Smooth, Craigo.

How much scarier is saying execute than simply kill? You can kill a keg of beer. But executing takes it to the next level. Craigo continues, but he lowers his voice a notch.

"I know PJ put you in a bad spot, and we'll do whatevah it takes to rectify that. I'm not gonna have yah face be a speed bag, just so you can pay yah weekly rent."

Veronica squirms to move the conversation off of Philip.

"Nah, you guys've been great. Suzanne calls every week, offering to look aftah Char. And you've got Philip all wrong. Sure, he's got a bit of a fiery tempeh, but he's a good bloke."

I grimace in disagreement. Craigo outpaces me.

"Why dontchya roll up yah sleeves? Show us how well stepfathah of the year treats you?"

She cowers and pulls away. Poor thing. Philip Morris has got to weigh a clean two thirty. Maybe more. And, being a cop, he's solid muscle.

"Craigo." I pop my eyes and give him a stern, yet respectful stare. It says, *chill the fuck out.* I turn to Veronica and soften my composure. Letting her know that I'm on her side.

"Veronica. We're…sorry. This is a lot. PJ's passing…it's been tough."

"I know. Fah me, too."

"Of course. And…I mean…imagine. Just over a week ago, I found out my best friend has a beautiful daughter. It's got us, especially me, all wound up."

"'Course. It's…" She doesn't know what to say. Good time for a joke.

"And thank god Charlotte has your cheeks and will have your nutritional standards. PJ's diet was horrific."

She cracks a smile.

Craigo follows.

A moment of unity. But it's brief.

Craigo nods toward a photo of Philip Morris.

"So, where is Mistah Charisma, anyway?"

"Training. The certification course in Canberra."

"When's he back?"

For a chubby boozehound, or pisshead as they say here, Craigo has an icy resolve.

"Not till aftah the weekend. He's going straight to Garie." She points to the photo of him and his pops surf fishing. "Bit of a bloke's weekend, othah than the last night. Saturday night."

"Oh, are you meeting him out there?"

"No, no. Saturday would've been his fathah's birthday. He'll go fishing alone. Spend the night on the piss. 'A cheers to the old man,' as he says."

"Mind if we pop 'round and say hello?"

•

"It was nice to see Charlotte, even though she was asleep."

"She's a doll."

"Ouch, fuck!"

"Yeah, the roll-bah gets cookin'. Watch yahself."

The Moke feels a lot smaller, with my arm crammed next to Craigo.

"Do you think she's cool with it?"

"With the intahvention? She wouldn't have told us where he was, all by himself, if it was a hard no."

"I know, but clearly she's not one to stand up for herself. I just worry that we're gonna put her in more jeopardy. I won't even be here in a week. I don't want to tinker with her life and then say 'see ya,' as I board the plane."

"Speak yah mind." He stops for a second. Drops his sarcasm. "You a'right being co-landlords with that twat?"

"Ugh. The thought of him being involved even 2% in the Surf School meets AirBnB extravaganza makes me furious. It was PJ's magnum opus."

"Magnum somethin'."

"No, I'm serious. I'm not being flippant. Who am I to come and try to pull some heroics? You have every right. And candidly, you are a straight up boss. I've never seen anyone so resolute. You know Philip Morris outweighs you by fifty pounds, right?"

"Pounds? Is this the Queen's English?"

"Sorry. Uhhh…" I try to calculate. "He outweighs you by twenty kilos. At least. What is that? Around four stone?"

"Not bad for an ignorant American." The roll bar has cooled. I hang my arms back up. Craigo continues. "But I don't undahstand yah question? The guy is violent. We have a sit down with him. He exits his relationship with my niece. And Vee. Immediately. Period. Or we escalate. Whether yah're here or not, it doesn't mattah. Doing nothing is not an option."

"You're right."

"It's a straightforward convahsation. I'll do the talking."

"What do I do?"

"Mate, yah're the muscle." He smirks.

I look at my scrawny arms. And my soft keyboard hands. Then I look over to Craigo. He turns the wheel of the Moke. He's got callouses. Muscle. Knuckles that'll be arthritic in a few decades.

"I'm in."

•

Long day.

Especially when you have a new girlfriend. Or, in my case, 50% new girlfriend, 50% old girlfriend.

I may give love advice for a living, but applying it to myself is nearly impossible. Nevertheless, whenever I'm an emotional train wreck, I must channel the energy and use it creatively. Shawna's asking if we can get back together has been haunting me. I pause thinking about her for a second and see if I can't repurpose the angst for work.

*@kafkasapple Every weekend, I think my girl and I are going to break up. But I*

*can't do it. I don't want to hurt her. How do I soften the blow?*

*@AskEsquire Be decisive and concrete. Say: I'm not in love with you. Sugarcoating it is like putting a disco ball on the pyramids—misleading & useless.*

You know how teachers always claim that they are unbiased when they grade papers? That the sweet kid doesn't get a better grade than the bully?

False.

For example: @kafkasapple has clearly read *The Metamorphosis*, making him a thoughtful, sensitive dude. Sure, maybe I'm wrong, but all I have to go on is his username and his question. So I give him the best advice I can give him. Even if the advice is tough. And I feel for him.

So sleepy.

•

I sleep for twenty minutes, but it feels like a year. The birds just woke up from a nap, too.

They used to sound sinister. Now they're my friends. I telepathically throw out a question. I ask them to weigh in on Shawna.

*Is thaaat my faaault? Naaah.*

Thanks, guys.

My Speedo sways over the bed. It looks dry. I tug at the earphone cord, hoping to pop it off, but it's too taut. Stupidly, I pull and pull and end up pulling myself off the bed. Holy shit this cord is strong. Bluetooth? I'll pass.

"Georgie, you up here?"

"Yeah, yeah. In my room."

"Hello love. I gotchya somethin'. Fah yah neck."

She pulls out a bottle of aloe.

"You are so thoughtful. It's…"

"Refreshing?"

"I was going to say undeserved. But yes, definitely refreshing."

"Just say thank you, Georgie. You don't have to ovahthink everything."

"Thank you. And perfect timing. I swam at Icebergs yesterday. My whole back got fried."

"Take yah shirt off, and lie down."

Suzanne starts with her hands on my neck. When you've just started having sex with someone, neither of you ever know when it's OK to initiate. Or if the first time was the last time.

Suzanne is cautious. I can't read her. But that last exchange with Shawna has me in a weird head space. I'm not sure if she senses this, but her touch hits the spot. She rubs my neck slowly, tenderly.

"Do you mind if I sit on top of you? Will it hurt?"

"Absolutely not."

She straddles me. It's innocent. She doesn't drop her full weight on me. She rubs the aloe into my back, thoroughly, turning it into a spa treatment. I wait a full two minutes, before I reach back and tuck my hands under her shins.

I need to stretch more.

She strokes my hands, telling me: *I wasn't sure if the other night was a one-night stand.*

I reach back further, stroking her feet, to let her know: *It wasn't.*

I roll over, onto my back. The moment I turn, she tugs at my shorts. Again, I'm not the most adept at picking up subtle cues.

A tornado of touching. Kisses that miss their targets but still land.

"Ah, oh. Ahhh. That feels…perfect."

Due to the wet aloe, the bottom fitted sheet is stuck to my back, like a sweaty batman's cape. I'm in her mouth. I don't want her to finish me. Not yet.

I grab her shoulders, pushing her away. But just her mouth. I shift her body, slide her shorts off and drop her hips onto mine.

She can feel that I'm close.

"Come inside me, Georgie."

And I do.

She slides off of me, gives me a quick kiss and slinks off to the bathroom. My exposed cock gives me the shivers. Coming inside a woman is surreal. It's divine, of course. But for me, it's complex, too. Shocking. In her mouth—she's literally devouring me. And inside of her? Her vagina? Sensually, it's magic. But no matter how safe she is or we are, it still feels like procreating. And that thought can be a mindfuck.

And I just came inside Suzanne.

She comes back with a towel for me.

"Are you sure you want me to use this?"

"Yeah, 'course. Why not?"

"It's nice. I don't use something this nice, when I'm, you know, by myself."

"If I needed to sort mahself out every day, I'd buy them in bulk, love."

"Ha. Good point. I do buy them in bulk. My socks."

"Georgie! I did not want to know that!"

"Just the clean ones. Sorry?"

"Nah, it's funny. Very juvenile, in a sweet way. And I'm not so naive. Why do you think Craigo keeps a box of tissues next to the computah at work?"

"Jesus. I did not want to know that."

She drops on top of me and pulls the covers over both of us. I look around the room at her framed sketches.

"It's so cool that you can draw. For someone who is snarky and pragmatic, I'd have never guessed that you're an artist."

"Didn't you just describe yahself?"

"No. I'm not an artist. Assembling quips is analytical. It only grazes being creative. I think it's what helps me appreciate what you can do. Because I can understand the openness. And the focus. Because I know, personally, how hard it is."

"What a charmah you are."

"Nah, it's true."

"What about yah girlfriend. Sharon? Isn't she artsy, too?"

"Shawna. You wanna talk about her again? After we just had sex? And she's not my girlfriend."

"Easy. I'm just curious. It doesn't bothah me. Girls aren't like blokes. We're not as territorial."

"That's not been my experience. Women are territorial. They're also curious. Maybe to a fault."

"Are you gendah stereotyping?"

"Stereotyping saves time."

"True, but it's a bit unfair. No?"

"Honestly, I have no idea. My job is to generalize. But it's for entertainment. Personally, I'm lost, when it comes to understanding women."

"Well played." She kisses me on the forehead. "So Shawna?"

"OK. Um…she studies art, but she's not an artist really. I guess we're similar in that way. The one thing that stands out about her, truly, is that she's an independent thinker. Her ability to digest new information, process it and respond with an original thought is impressive. She's awful to argue with. It's like bringing a knife to a gunfight."

"Oh dear."

"It's a lot. It was a lot. But it can be intoxicating, too."

"Were you in love?"

"I was. I don't think I am anymore. And it's unfair to her. Because she thinks she holds me up. It's recent, but she has put me on some sort of weird pedestal."

"Is that so terrible?"

"It's unnerving to be treated like that. I used to worship her. Then, the moment I didn't, our power balance flipped. To be given someone's total submission. It's…"

"Ovahwhelming?"

"Exactly."

"How do you see her now?"

"Honestly?"

"Yeah."

"I see her as a crutch. I hate myself for it, but I do. Trust me, she's done her share of damage, too."

"Now that is a lot."

"Suzanne, I want to be transparent. I did just email her a few days ago. We're not together, but we're still in touch."

"Feel free to be a bit less transparent. Sometimes honesty doesn't do us any favahs."

"I'm sorry, I…"

"Georgie. We've both had a traumatic life event. That's what crutches are for. Shall we drop this topic? Give us a kiss. And go make me a cup of tea. We'll pretend it was yah idea."

•

8am.

We're in the kitchen chatting, and I'm heading out to get a coffee. I think of all of the times I've heard people say: *We're taking it slow*. And I think of what a crock of shit that is, for me. I envy the ability to execute that cadence. We had another bone session in the middle of the night. This morning? I made her bed. I've never been on a first date that didn't last three years.

"Are you going to see Charlotte in the next few days? Before Craigo and I go out to Garie?"

"Yeah, eithah today or tomorrow. Vee wanted to get a pedicure while Philip's away."

"At their house?"

"Yeah?"

"Can you do something for me? Take a look at the cache on her computer? Look at her browser history?"

"Why?"

"I want to know if she actually wants help. If she's seeking an exit."

"That seems a bit…invasive?"

"She didn't say much when Craigo and I were there. She just looked afraid. I wanna get in her head. The best way to do that is to get into her computer. See what she's looking at."

"Sneaky." She kisses me. "Alright then. Why don't you come yahself?"

"Would that be OK?"

"'Course. Plus you could get a little more time with Charlotte, before you go."

Every day that I don't book a flight brings me closer to spending Christmas Down Under. Because I used the *Esquire* corporate account (relax, I paid for it), I only booked one way. It's a small perk that allows me to book a relatively cheap flight home, refundable, without any penalties. Working for the man has its privileges. But it's mid-December, and if I put it off another week, it'll be another Christmas without seeing my mom. Plus, I might end up with a wife that has an accent.

"Yeah. I need to book that ticket. Hey do you want a piccolo or…?"

"Yes, please." She tickles her hand down my back and heads upstairs.

We're discussing me leaving, but she voluntarily departs the conversation, herself.

# 8

9am.

Bronte, at Christmas, reminds me of an El Niño winter in LA. It's a ninety-second walk to Favoloso, and I'm already squinting without sunglasses. It's hot. Even the sparse Christmas lights on the Aussie townhouse balconies look like they're sweating.

"Georgie!"

"Gosso. What's the word?"

He's wearing a goofy Santa hat. It's makes him even more attractive.

Impossible.

"We've gotta get you some bettah fitting boardies, mate. You look like you stepped right outta the Elle Bee Cee."

"Do you understand as little of what I say, as I do of you? I'm lucky to comprehend 50%. No offense. And these shorts do fit.

They're snug at the waist and within an inch of my knee. Read any fashion blog."

He whips behind the counter, sporting a pair of very short, pastel shorts. They show off his muscular quads.

"The Elle Bee Cee? You nevah listened to Sublime? Forty Ounces 'a' Freedahm?"

"Oh, the LBC. How do you even know that? And trust me, you don't want to see my chicken legs in those shorts. But your 90's hip-hop knowledge is truly game-show worthy. It's embarrassing how little I know about Australia by comparison. Nicole Kidman?"

"What do you Yanks know about Oz?"

"Uhhh, Ned Kelly, Captain Cook, Empire of the Sun, Margot Robbie and Hugh Jackman? Beyond that, absolutely nothing."

"Nice one! That's 500% more than the othah sepos!" Sepo = slang for septic—Australian cockney for Septic Tank Yank.

"Yeah, but I have an advantage. I lived with an Aussie for a year."

"And yah're all at a massive disadvantage, given that the majority of mass media originates in the States. It's not yah fault yah're egocentric. You don't have the exposah; you don't know any bettah."

"That's gracious, even if you are enabling our ignorance."

"Yah're welcome. It must be odd, everywhere you go, to have a non-reciprocal cultural exchange. Everyone knows yah Pressie, but you guys haven't got a clue who our PM is."

He's right. We don't.

"Scott Morris?"

"Scott Morrison."

"Sorry. Have you thought about being a pop culture professor, maybe housed in a philosophy department at a university? You're missing your calling."

"Who would froth the milk fah yah bird? And I'm not talking about the bird in the tree."

•

---

**From:** Rogers, Timothy

**To:** Lewis, George

**Subject:** Workload

George—

I've been reading your Tweets. They seem to be coming along nicely. I did want to check in on your workload. I'm not sure how long it takes to navigate the queue (the last time I opened it up, it was daunting, as you said), but if you are interested and have the time, we might be able to offer you some other pieces to work on.

To be clear—I'm not looking to add work—what you're doing now is great. But once you're back in the States, you might want to consider adding some longer elements to your portfolio. As a Staff Writer, you get bonus pay for incremental publications.

Just a thought.

Looking forward to connecting with you in the New Year.

TR

PS While you are in Australia, try to catch a glimpse of the Southern Cross. It should be an easy one, but it's been sitting on my bucket list for ages.

---

The Southern Cross is the Big Dipper of the southern hemisphere. TR is a thoughtful guy. Pretty cool of him to think of me expanding my portfolio.

My iMessage pops.

Shawna.

---

You there?

Hey. Yeah, I'm here. Just got up.

Sorry I didn't email you back.

No worries. Feels like I just wrote you.

Do you have a second? I need to chat with you about something.

Uh, sure. Do you want me to call you? I can pop by the shop in a few hours and call you from there?

No, it's late here, and I'm at my mom's.
I don't want to wake her up.

Cool. I just gotta motor fairly soon.
Going to babysit Charlotte.
What's up?

I'm late.

Like late, late?

Yeah.

Are you OK?

I'm a little freaked out.

We should talk on the phone.
Can you, later?

Yeah, maybe tomorrow. I keep
hoping to get my period. It's always
been sporadic and often late. Just
never this late before. And I never,

ever forget to take my fucking pill.

Yeah, you're pretty religious about
it.

Remember how I had that sore throat
forever, before I came to Panama?

Yeah?

After three different medications,
my doc prescribed Rifampin.

OK?

Rifampin is one of the few antibiotics
that neutralizes the effectiveness of the pill.

Oh.

Maybe she mentioned it?
It seems like something I
would have remembered.

There's no way she mentioned it.
You're always so on top of

everything.

I was so, so sick. And obviously
not having sex. I'm so sorry, George.

No, no it's OK. It takes
two to tango. It's not on
you.

To be clear, this is not 100% confirmed.
But something is off. I'm getting a
blood test, if I don't get my period in
the next few days.

I'm sorry, I don't mean to
micromanage, I'm just curious:
have you done one of those
stick things?

No. And before you judge,
I have done them before. When
we were first dating, and I got a false
positive. I want to go to a doc and be
for sure, for sure. You know?

Of course. Are you OK?

You've got a lot going on.
I wish I was there.

Are YOU OK? Is this freaking
YOU out?

It is a bit shocking. But nothing
surprises me these days.
I just wanna make sure you are
OK and don't feel alone.

I hate how calm you are in a crisis.
Seriously, it drives me crazy. But thank you.
Hearing your voice, even virtually,
is the calmest I've felt in a few days.

Yeah, yeah. Let's talk live, OK?
Plus I'm off to babysit. Maybe
it'll be good practice?

Not funny.

Zero funny?

A little funny. Fucker.

OK. Hang in there. I'll call you
from the shop in the afternoon,
your tomorrow morning.

OK. Thank you George. Maybe
I'm being an alarmist, but I feel
way better now that I told you.
Waaay better.

I'm glad.

Sigh. Thank you. I love you
(you don't have to say it back).

I love you too. I'll catch you
tomorrow. Just chill and we'll
figure it out. OK?

Thank you. So much.
OK. Talk to you tomorrow.

Night, Shawna.

---

Deep exhale. Another.

Poor thing. A few things that run through my mind, because I am a terrible person:

1. Are you sure it's mine?
2. Really sure?
3. What are we gonna do?
4. What are you gonna do?
5. Please please please that say your career is important to you or that you think I'd be a bad dad or that you're not ready or that Parkinson's runs in your family or whatever reason you want but that there is no question—you've made an appointment at Planned Parenthood to get an abortion.

Birth Control. Planned Parenthood. Both misnomers. Should be renamed: Birth Avoidance and Unplanned Parenthood.

I should walk into Suzanne's room and tell her.

But, on second thought, if Shawna's not actually pregnant, that could be really mean. Doing nothing is, occasionally, the best option. And the worst feeling.

I burn time by defaulting to work.

Flipping through the queue, nothing seems to resonate. I don't know if I have the chops to write a pithy response to my own quandary:

*@georgeiscompletelyfucked 2 girls. 1 pregnant. Help?*

•

"Georgie? You in there?"

"Yeah, yeah."

She pops her head in the doorway.

"Sorry, I'm not quite ready. Give me ten?"

"Nah, you've got heaps of time. It's only been a few minutes."

"It feels like a lifetime." Or however long it takes to go from not being a dad to maybe being a dad.

"A lifetime? Okaaay…Anyways, I wasn't sure if you'd booked yah flight yet, and I wanted to make sure you'd save some room in yah suitcase for a little pressie—before you fill it up with Bronte SLSC swag."

Smart. I'm currently wearing the Surf Life Saving Club hoodie I bought the morning Santa greeted the Nippers.

She slides me a small rectangular gift. I open it. It's a professionally framed drawing of the Bronte Baths.

"Wow, Suzanne. It's perfect. I love it. How'd you get the aerial perspective?"

"Google satellite image, love."

"Oh."

The first semi-gift that Shawna ever gave me was a hand-drawn bookmark of the YMCA pool, where I used to give swim lessons. Shawna's not a practiced artist like Suzanne. She was just expressing a sentiment in a charming way—her interest to go on our first date.

To attempt to represent the world, through my eyes, is a great act of love. It humbles me. And breaks my heart a little.

An appropriate thank you would be a long kiss. But I can't think of anything more disingenuous, than engaging Suzanne physically, moments after Shawna's revelation. Instead, I dive into her work.

"You double inked the whole thing?"

"How'd you know?"

"I saw you doing it the other day. It's part of your style—makes the corners really sharp, like it was etched into stone."

"Well that's the goal, at least."

"How long did this take?"

"Bloody ages."

"Your interpretation of it is so real. It's more real than the real thing. How do you do that?"

"Dunno. Just by looking, I guess."

"Plus talent. Plus skill. Plus a boatload of practice."

She stops and thinks, taking the question seriously.

"I guess, if you look at something long enough, you don't just see it visually. You start to see how it feels. That's what I try to draw."

"That is such a great description."

"Isn't it the same? With words?"

"I guess."

"Pick something. In this room. And describe it. I'd like to watch."

"Right now?"

"Please."

I stare back at her.

"Can I cheat, a little?"

"'Course."

"Do you remember picking me up from the airport? The moment we first got into your little car?"

"Yeah?"

"I wrote a note about that moment. About you. Knowing I'd want to use its essence someday."

"What was it?"

"There's a warmth in her eyes that could break a clock."

# 9

I'm finally getting the hang of getting in on the passenger side of the car. But I still look the wrong way, as we pull out of the driveway.

"I like your car. Efficient. Functional."

"Dontchya all drive utes in the States?"

"We're coming around. From what I've seen here, cars cost 50% more. Gas costs 50% more. You guys had to cut short the infatuation with subsidized gas-guzzlers. I will not lie; I'm a little weak for any American car made before 1970. But we paid for the SUV bonanza in every way—psychologically, environmentally, not to mention homeland security."

"Oh, my little mental Georgie." She drops me a sideways smile and taps my knee. Time to get off my soapbox and say something nice.

"I know we are having a weird whirlwind romance under exceptional circumstances, but I do want to say this: you are way too fucking beautiful to be as kind, easygoing, humble and whip smart as you are."

"Do you always curse, in yah flattery?"

"Fuck. Sorry."

"I'm just teasing love, thank you. That is so sweet. And quite an original compliment, I must say."

She taps her cheek for a kiss.

•

"Shhh. She finally dozed off."

Veronica has Charlotte in one of those new age baby wrap things. It's a replica of the cloth female farmers used to (and probably still do) wrap their babies in, while working in the fields throughout Asia and South America. Now it's fully branded, organic and for sale in twelve colors at Jack n Jill.

We huddle and whisper.

"Is she ever not asleep?"

"She's a newborn!"

"Trust me, she's often not. But she is a good baby. Was just fussing a bit this afternoon. But now she'll sleep fah a few hours."

Suzanne looks relieved.

"So nice of you two to come watch her."

"Nah, thanks for letting us. It's nice to see her, even sleeping." I lean in, drop a soft kiss on her forehead and drink in her scent. "I can't get over her baby's breath."

"Well, she's got some not so nice smells coming out of her elsewhere." Veronica drops her eyes to Charlotte's diaper. "Don't judge a book by its covah."

We giggle. Baby number two jokes are always a hit.

"Hey love? Mind if we use a computah or two while we babysit?"

And to think I thought she only called me *love.* But I appreciate her being proactive with our little covert plan.

"Yeah, 'course. My Mac is in the kitchen. It's not locked. If you both need to do a bit of work at the same time, Philip's laptop is in the study. His password is Victoria Bitter, spelled with the number 3 for the e. All one word. Capital V, capital B. A bit blokey, but easy to remembah!"

His password is basically: *BudL!ght.*

"Sheeehhhm." Charlotte lets out a sleepy sigh. So cute.

"That's my cue! Let me go put her down. Fix yahselves a drink or somethin'!"

We meander around the kitchen, not sure what to do. I'm starting to get a bit nervous, but I'm more curious than anything. And Veronica's computer is sitting right there.

"She's in a good mood."

"Char?"

"No. Vee. Way more calm and smiley than last time."

"Because that bloody wank has been outah her hair for a few days."

"What she sees in him, I have no idea."

"Agreed. Even his password indicates that he's a bloody idiot."

I open the fridge and, to bring her point home, pull out a Victoria Bitter.

"Do you mind? While in Rome."

"You'd drink a VB?"

I open it.

"Yeah? I think they're good."

Suzanne is not impressed.

Veronica returns, looking cute. Flowy top. Stretch pants. A barrette in her hair that gives her a little edge, while maintaining her femininity. She looks more vibrant, happier. Especially minus the mom gear. The silk scarf looks natural; you wouldn't think it's hiding the last day of a bruise.

"George, we've got Toohey's in the car park. Don't drink that!"

"No, no, I'm good."

Suzanne rolls her eyes at Veronica. A shared moment between two women. Men—no need for words.

VB tastes good. Haters.

"You look nice, love!"

"Aw, hardly. This is the only thing that fits. But it is nice to have a bit of makeup on. Feel like a real woman again! And I can't thank you enough for watching Char. I haven't had my nails done in ages."

"Our pleasure. Go! Enjoy yahself! Sit and have a coffee. Did you want one of these?" Suzanne pulls out a few magazines from her bag. Veronica grabs one bashfully, like a Mennonite touching an iPhone.

I get it.

Why PJ had a thing for her.

She's so, so sweet.

Even though he was a womanizer, PJ had excellent taste.

•

E-cigs aren't the only thing trying to poison Philip Morris. Veronica's browser history is an absolute tell-all. Marriage Act of 1961. Implications of de facto marriage (common law). Common law, in New South Wales, is enforcable at two years of cohabitation. Such a soft interpretation in California would cripple the court system.

She's done pretty extensive research on domestic violence conviction rates. Domestic violence average prison sentences. Here's the kicker—she's looked at more than ten sites that detail how to make cyanide at home. She also dabbled in arsenic acquisition, but Veronica really honed in on cyanide. Cyanide—apricot pit versus apple seeds—how to make it in the kitchen.

Good job, Internet.

Apple seeds were the clear winner. There's a page-full of sites. I turn and look at the fruit bowl. Four Granny Smiths look innocuous and lethal.

I glance at Suzanne. She's drawing on the edge of a magazine, just a few feet from me. Her lines are precise. They look three dimensional.

"Well, Veronica is way more stressed out about Philip Morris than she lets on. She's got enough domestic violence research here to stock a women's shelter. And she's no stranger to 'how to make household poison in three easy steps.'"

"Oh dear."

"But seeing her today? I doubt she'd go through with anything that drastic."

"Cyanide apple pie?"

"How do you know that?"

"Crime series on the telly. But the sheer quantity of apple seeds makes it unrealistic. Othahwise, there'd be a lot of dead blokes, now wouldn't there?"

"Wow. That joke came a little too quick. Still, it says a lot about her mindset. We're not overreacting. She must feel like she has nowhere to turn."

Charlotte mumbles on the baby monitor.

"Poor thing. Lemme go check on Char."

"Cool. I'm gonna pop the hood on Philip's computer, just for grins."

•

*VictoriaBitt3r.*

Dude, seriously?

Philip Morris's computer is older than Veronica's Mac. But his browser history is clean clean clean. He's a male; so that's not such a big deal. No girlfriend or spouse wants proof that most men are addicted to porn.

I do an image search and increase the file size results, narrowing it down to only high-resolution pictures.

Tons of photos show him fishing. Gun range. Drinking. Bro fest. Repeat.

I scroll and scroll.

Nothing here.

Hmmm.

Not a single photo of an old girlfriend in a bikini? That's not believable. I go to the folder options menu and select *Display Hidden*

*Files.*

Search again.

Bingo.

There's a thumbnail of a naked female.

I double click.

It's a girl. A child. Under twelve.

"Oh god."

The surroundings are a dingy hotel room. An accurate brochure for sex tourism.

I look at the file location, and it's deep under the archives, in a *Taxes* folder. Double click. Whoa.

It's a chronicle of sex with young girls. Naked. On their knees. No smiles.

Philip Morris has been raping young girls for a long time. Years and years. The Philippines, Indonesia, Malaysia. There are a few interspersed fishing photos.

And he's not alone. His buddies are doing it with him.

"Jesus."

Suzanne pops her head in.

"She's fast asleep."

"Uhhh…"

"Whattaya doing?"

"You don't wanna see this."

"Is that what Phil has been up to?"

"Yeah, for ages. Trips everywhere. Even Micronesia."

"Oh my god, I think I'm gonna be sick."

"Join the club."

"Then why do you keep looking at them? Shut that thing down."

"I'm trying to find something more incriminating. Like a photo with him in it…"

"Like that. Disgusting."

"Yep."

In one of the recent sets of photos, Philip is taking a selfie, with a young girl servicing him.

Fucking pedophile rapist nostril flarer.

"Georgie. Let's just go."

"What?"

"Let's take Charlotte and get outta here."

"Oh."

"I'm not kidding."

"I know. I know."

"I don't have a car seat, but…" I cut her off.

"Suzanne, I totally agree with you. Totally. But we can't kidnap her. We'd never get to see her again. And we'd make this so much worse. I promise you that we'll figure out a way to punish Philip Morris. But we can't be impetuous. And Craigo is right. The first step is getting him away from her and this house."

"How?"

"We're already going to talk to him at Garie. Now? We give him an ultimatum. Given that he's a cop, I don't know how we can get him arrested, yet. But we can certainly scare him. Scare him out of coming back here. At least in the short term. That has to be enough. For now."

"This. Is. Bloody. Infuriating." She looks at the photos. "And whattaya gonna do with those? You do not want to send those to yahself."

"I'm just gonna take some screenshots. I doubt it'd hold up in court, but it's better than nothing. I figure if I can show a screenshot of this, and a few others, it'll at least be something. Maybe I'll look in the settings and see if I can grab a screenshot of his computer's serial number. Put it side by side with one of the photos."

"Alright. I guess it's a good idea? The whole thing makes me want to vomit. And yah're putting yahself at risk by even tinkering with those. Bloody wank."

"I know. It's sketchy. But doing nothing is not an option. I was trying to think of a way to get one of those Proof of Life hostage photos, with the kidnapee and today's paper, but the information age makes that totally irrelevant."

"How do you come up with this stuff? I'm going back to look at beautiful Charlotte, to cleanse my soul. Then, I'll head out to the kitchen and be yah 'lookout'. Do whatchya think is best. Just be quick about it."

"Good call. Thanks."

"And take a look on the left, on his desktop. Is that a receipt or something?"

I open it.

"It's a receipt for E-cigs. He buys them online?"

"They're not sold here. At least not with nicotine. Not yet. That receipt is yah Proof of Life, Mr. Superspy. Include that in one of yah screenshots."

•

"Suzie Q!"

"Craigo, it's George. I'm using Suzanne's phone."

"Aw mate, was just thinkin' about you. Yestdahday, I popped into Hardware fah a quick bite."

"Yeah. I've been meaning to eat there. Such a great name for a bar. Anyway, listen, I…" He cuts me off, excited to share some tidbit.

"So, I'm in the toilet, and this idiot pulls out his phone at the urinal."

"OK?"

"The urinal! Can't even take a piss without it!"

"I think it's psychosomatic."

"Ay?"

"What percent of guys use their phones for porn?"

"Ahhh, ninety-five?"

"At least. They're so used to grabbing their phone, whenever they're touching their dick, it feels natural in a public restroom."

I grimace. This quip feels a little too close and too soon, given my afternoon.

"Savages. Hey, come pick you up? I'm heading up to Bondi Road for a bottle of piss. Good timing on the call."

"Wait. Stop. I'm getting distracted. Just listen, OK?"

"Fire away."

"I can't hang out. I'm at Veronica's. That's why I called."

"You guys watching Char? Yah're practically settin' up house togethah!" He thinks his own joke is really funny. An affliction I also suffer from.

"Just listen. I snooped around Philip's computer. He's got tons of photos with him and kids. All from trips he took throughout Asia. They're not nice photos, Craigo. It's awful. These girls are young. Preteen."

"Mothah…fuckah."

"I don't know what to do. He needs to go to prison. But I have no idea how to navigate that here. But we should keep our plan. Definitely confront him at Garie tomorrow."

"Didjya captcha any evidence?"

"Yeah. But it's weak. I'm no computer scientist. I just took some screenshots. But it'll definitely be enough to scare him."

"Good boy. OK. Let's hit Garie tomorrow. Catch the wank by himself, with nowhere to run."

"Yeah. Agreed."

"I'll grab you in the pm, 'round three."

"Hey, and do you mind if I cruise by the shop on the way home? I need to make a few calls to the States. It'd cost a fortune from Suzanne's phone."

"'Course, mate. And print off whatevah you've got on Philip. We'll shove it undah his nose tomorrow."

"Do you think our first step should be to go to the cops?"

"Do you?"

"I don't know. He is a fucking cop. And based on the photos, it looks like he's going on these trips with other cops. Who could we trust?"

"How can you tell they're cops?"

"Their haircuts."

"Right."

"You were right at the bar. Keeping him away from Charlotte is the first step. We can figure out how to lock him up later. Poor Vee. I can't imagine."

"Agreed. One thing at a time. Let's just first get him the bloody hell away from my niece. We can pursue the criminality anothah day."

"Yeah, yeah. OK. I think so, too."

"A'right. Catchya latah. I'm gonna pack up a few things, hit the piss and crash early. You should do the same."

"Craigo, it's so fucked up. These girls. Their eyes. It's haunting."

"Undahstood, mate. Imagine being a fathah."

"I know. I know."

"Well, we've got our work cut out fah us. Get a good night's sleep, a'right? Tight lines."

# 10

"You don't want me to wait? Or come back?"

"Nah, I've gotta make a few phone calls. Print some stuff. Need to check in on work, too. I can just walk up the hill. No biggie."

"OK."

I can't put my finger on it, but Suzanne almost looks deflated.

"Would you mind grabbing us some food? I'll be famished, by the time I'm back. It'd be nice to eat takeout and watch a movie or something?"

"'Course, love. I'll grab something yummy fah takeaway and check out what's On Demand. See you in a bit."

I bank another one, for the next time I'm dry:

*@AskEsquire Want to know how your girl feels about you? Ask her a favor.*

The two cashiers at WGB wave me through to Craigo's office without incident. As if I was doing them a favor. All customer service training should be conducted in Australia.

"Hi Shawna. How are you? Things good? How's carrying my baby?"

Not my best practice run, aloud, as I hold my hand over the receiver. I'm still too gun-shy to dial.

I fire up Craigo's shop computer and print off the Philip pedophile and rape evidence. Just touching the warm printouts makes me cringe.

On Craigo's desktop, he's got a document titled: *Georgie Stuff*. I open it, since respect for another's privacy is a complete wash for today. My t-shirt and card ideas are all neatly spelled out. Pretty rad, Craigo.

I've got a few more for him. To save a step, I type them underneath:

Three hand gestures, indicating a sign language phrase. Translated in small font underneath: *Sorry I mumble.*

*The oil companies don't get enough credit for saving the whales.*

*Sorry my breath smells like booze. That's just what it smells like.*

*Patriot & idiot both end with the same three letters, but they don't have to be synonyms, idiot.*

Hopefully he'll get a chuckle when I'm gone.

I need to book my flight.

But I need to do this first.

OK.

Let's do it.

Two misdials.

Why is it so difficult to dial internationally?

*Ring, ring.*

"George?"

"Shawna?"

"Heeey. Oh my god, how are you? So nice to hear your voice."

"Yeah, thanks. More importantly, how are you?"

"I'm good. Everything cool with PJ's family? You feel good? Like you got closure?"

"Yeah, well. Sort of. I think I will. There are more loose ends than I expected."

"Makes sense."

"Really? Why?"

"The soul of another is a dark forest. PJ was a vibrant expressive guy. Just not emotionally. It's not surprising."

"Applying Russian proverbs to PJ is oddly poetic."

"Learned it from you, snarkmonster."

"Ha. Fair." It's a bummer we can't catch up. She never lets me get away with anything. And, sometimes, I enjoy it. But that's not why we're on the phone. "Sooo…should we talk about…"

"Yeeeah. Hey, do you have dependent care at Esquire? Because I think the Montessori kindergarten I picked is gonna be pricey."

She howls with laughter.

"You are so fucked up."

"You mean knocked up."

"Yet another topic navigated with grace."

"George, I'm two weeks late. And I'm freaking out. Freaking. The. Fuck. Out."

"I can imagine. It's good you're going to the doc."

"Totally. I got antsy and already called. My gyno's out of town, but she's back in a few days. I'm already booked. I could go to someone else, but…"

"Nah, it's so personal. It makes sense to go to someone you trust."

"Could not agree more." She sighs. "Are you not freaked out? Why are you so calm? It's annoying."

"I'm trying to be supportive. I don't know what to say?"

"George just…"

"Shawna. It's crazy. I feel a mix of emotions. But I also feel one overwhelming one. That I want you to feel that I'm here. That I'm by your side. That we'll figure this out. OK? I'm coming home in a week. You don't need to do a single thing until then. Just hang tight, and we'll figure it out."

"You are? Coming home?"

"I'm gonna book my flight right now. It'll be at some terrible time, because I waited too long, and I'll probably have to fly home on Christmas Day, but I will book it the moment I get off the phone. OK?"

"Thank you. Not sure exactly why, but that does make me feel better."

"I'll forward you the itinerary as soon as it's booked."

"I guess you didn't picture a stroller under the tree?"

"And she's back. What is the ratio? One minute of feeling fragile and sensitive to an hour of biting sarcasm?"

"Tell me you'd want it the other way around."

"White flag. I surrender."

"Hee hee."

"You sound better. I'm glad we talked."

"Me too, George. I miss…"

I cut this off.

"Hey, I should probably go? I'm calling from the shop, and it can't be cheap."

Lie.

"Oh! Of course! OK! See you soon, sweetie!"

"Bye Shawna."

•

*@stopmattresspricewars My gf is pregnant. How do I tell her I want her to get an abortion, nicely?*

*@AskEsquire You don't. You can't. Tell her you love her. Stay by her side. It's her body. Support her. That's all you can do.*

Do I want Shawna to get an abortion?

Yes.

Does admitting that make me feel awful?

Yes.

Do I also have mixed feelings about bringing another being into the world, after looking at tens of young girls being raped by a cop?

Yes.

You'd need a new word for yes. Because yes doesn't cover it. Not even close.

•

"Georgie, didju want some poppies?"

Suzanne is teeing up a nice romantic night for us and yelling upstairs—asking how best to please me. I needed some air after talking to Shawna. Took the long way home from the shop. Now, I'm trying to finish up some work. The number of pregnancy fear questions in the Twitter queue is nearly unlimited. No wonder Dr. Drew had such a fruitful career on *Loveline*.

"Sure. Can I have another twenty minutes?"

"Take yah time, love."

Her being sweet makes me feel terrible.

I should tell her.

Instead, I'm gonna book my flight. And insert half of the earth between us.

LAX to SYD: 17 hour time difference (loss) + 15 hour flight = you leave one night and land in the morning, two days later. SYD to LAX: 17 hour time difference (gain) + 14 hour flight (an hour faster, due to the trade winds) = you arrive the same day, a few hours earlier. Isn't that insane?

Because Christmas day was the only day left to fly, I'll be spending Christmas on two continents. With both of my girlfriends.

---

**From:** Georgeous

**To:** Shawna B.

**Subject:** FW: united.com reservation for Los Angeles, California (LAX)

shawna—
heyo. scroll way, way down for my itinerary.

sorry i land on christmas day. the early bird gets the worm. the late bird gets the middle seat?

please graciously accept the dinner offer from your mom. i get in super early, so i'll probably spend the day with my mom. let me know what time to come over and what to bring. i know your mom loves the fancy box wine.
g
ps oddly excited for the LA version of winter and wearing long sleeves, pants and flip-flops. you cannot fathom how hot it is here, even compared to panama.

---

**From:** Lewis, George

**To:** Rogers, Timothy

**Subject:** RE: Workload

Tim—

Thanks for your note. I would love to work on another piece. The Tweets are good—sometimes quick to write, other times not, but I could certainly take on a bit more, especially if the deadline is flexible.

And I won't write run-on sentences like that last one. I promise.

Two work items on this same thread:

1. Have you thought about expanding to Instagram? We could duplicate the Tweets or use it as a completely different channel—aka tell a different story.
2. I've always wanted to do something on life skills. We could start with a complete idiot (myself) and learn to tie sailor's knots, rebuild a car engine, etc. It'd be a series—from novice to expert—over a period of time.

A lot will depend on where I decide to live.
Anyway, just a few thoughts. Take them or leave them.

Best,
George

PS I may be far enough away from the city tomorrow night to see the Southern Cross—thanks for the suggestion.

---

Life Skills Volume One: *How do you make a 230lb prick disappear?* Suzanne yells up the stairs, again.

"Georgie, do you want buttah?"

"Sure. I'm almost done. Be right down."

PJ used to love the fully loaded popcorn. Leave it to people with six-pack abs to eat like shit. Suzanne hasn't completed ten seconds of exercise since I've been here; yet she's got the muscle tone of an athlete.

"Did you pick something?"

"I was thinking that Kurt Vonnegut semi-documentary?"

"A Man Without a Country? Are you taking a jab?"

"Ay?"

"Sorry, the title hits a little close to home."

"Ah, gotchya. Something simpler, a bit more Chrissy? Like *Elf*?"

"Perfect."

"You seem edgy, love. Worried about tomorrow?"

"Yeah, a couple of things. I booked my flight. I haven't been home in so long, I don't know where to start. And dealing with Philip is kinda freaking me out."

"'Course. I've been thinking about it, too. Honestly, love, I was restless fah a few hours. But I feel a lot bettah knowing that he is isolated out at Garie. And that we aren't going to let him get away with it. Knowing that you and Craigo are doing something tomorrow—it comforts me a bit."

"I'm glad. Wish I could say the same."

"You'll just have a chat with him, tell him he is no longah welcome within a thousand kilometers of Charlotte or Vee, that a warrant is forthcoming and come home."

"And I'm sure that'll go smoothly. 'Oh, hey bro. You're a pedophile. And a woman beater. Why don't you skip town?'"

"Of course it will go terribly, but he needs to know he has eyes on him. Just that is a step in the right direction."

"I'm always impressed by people that can capture everything I feel and distill it down into two sentences."

"Why dontchya capture those watah glasses and distill them onto the coffee table."

"Bam. But you're right. I guess if we keep it that simple, it should be OK."

"It's good yah're here. Othahwise, I'm pretty sure Craigo would kill him."

"Not sure that I'd stop him."

She kisses me on the forehead.

"When's yah flight?"

"Christmas Day. Brutal. But that's all that was left. And I need to get home, it's…"

"'Course. Yah family must miss you. You gonna spend Chrissy with yah mum?"

"Yeah. I need to send her an email. Generally, I try not to tease her. I've been gone a long time."

"Fear of commitment. From a bloke? Shocking."

She munches a handful of popcorn. I keep waiting for the bomb. *What about us? Dontchya think we have a futah togethah?*

But she doesn't. And, I realize, of the two of us, I'd be the one asking this question.

"What time's the departure?"

"Just before noon. I get there at 6am. Double Christmas."

"Oh, that's good! You'll be here for Christmas eve. Bloody hell! I need to pull the tree out of the garage!"

"An artificial tree?"

"Yeah, a bit antiseptic, but I hated having to cut down a tree every year."

"I could not agree more. What kind of holiday tradition supports cutting down a tree? It's the worst messaging. Even stupid Valentine's Day is better, with binge eating chocolate."

"And cut down flowahs."

"You're right. Both stupid. Celebration is apparently a synonym for pointless consumption."

"Let's watch the movie, love. Yah're getting all wound up ovah nothing. Toss us the blanket, and let me stick my feet under you. They're freezing."

•

*Elf* puts me to sleep. It's amazing how quickly we become creatures of habit. Suzanne's shirt is off before we reach the top of the stairs. I head to my room, take off my jeans and hear the birds.

"*Is thaaat my bra straaap…naaah.*" Even the birds know I'm racked with guilt over my two girlfriends. In self-critique, the guilt really only kicked in with Shawna's recent revelation, since she is technically my ex-girlfriend. Still, admitting that, if only to myself, makes it sting a little worse.

I sit on the bed and drop my head. My mind spirals into a bizarre daydream, where I'm shopping for a crib, and Suzanne sends me a text:

*Georgie! Hope all is well stateside. Sending some love your way. Sx*

It could not feel more realistic.

"Georgie? You coming?" Suzanne stands in the doorway.

"Ah!"

"Did I scare you?"

"Yeah. Sorry. Zoned out."

"Why dontchya come tah bed?"

She's naked, other than lacy boy-short panties. If I didn't know the meaning of the word: *irresistible*, I do now.

"I feel a little weird." Don't worry; I'm not gonna tell her about the possible bun in the oven.

"Are you ill?" She walks over and reaches down, placing her hand on my cheek. It's so sweet. And the fact that she's almost naked makes it more sincere.

"No, no. Not ill. I just feel a little weird. With us, you know…"

"That yah're shagging yah dead best friend's sistah?" My eyes pop. Speechless. "Let's just call it what it is, love."

"No, I don't. I'm not. I didn't come here to…" She cuts me off.

"It's OK, Georgie. Not sure that I'd add this tactic to yah advice column. But I'm a big girl. And you've not made a single move that wasn't already welcomed. Don't ovahthink it."

"Yeeeah."

"Come. Let's go tah bed. I'm a bit knackered, anyway. We can renegotiate in the morning."

She tugs at my hand, and I follow her into her bedroom. She's made every excuse for me and could not have been kinder. The result? I feel worse. And it's deserved.

We climb into bed.

In moments, she's dozing. She smells minty, and cuddling into her is welcoming. She backs up into me—another part of our rhythm.

She mumbles, sweetly.

"Left you some watah, beside thah bed."

"I saw. Thank you."

I kiss her shoulder.

Women rarely write in to @AskEsquire. And when they do, they rarely ask specific questions. It's usually something broad and unanswerable like: *Why are men such cheating assholes?* At least unanswerable in a short Tweet. But, occasionally, when they're not broad, females' questions tend to be more poignant and concrete than males'. And I like to have a few at the ready, like:

*@fictitiousfemale I've been on four dates with this guy. I like him. But I'm not ready for sex. I've blown him, but I worry that's not enough?*

*@AskEsquire It's more than enough. Just the fact that you want to touch him will keep him on the hook for weeks.*

Bang. Yet another future life altered, at least temporarily, in two sentences. You'd be surprised what it takes to get them this short.

Sometimes, I'll waste ten minutes trying to get a twenty-word bit down to eighteen. I have no idea if it's worth it, or if anyone cares, but that doesn't stop me.

Suzanne turns and kiss-bites me. It's aggressive. I was liking her plan of allowing me to torment myself all night and coming up with some other reason to not sleep with her by the morning. The task I failed to complete during Will Ferrell's finest hour (zero sarcasm, *Elf* is genius).

"Suzanne, just…"

"Shhh."

She grabs my cock. It has betrayed me, by being painfully erect.

She puts me in her mouth and pulls at me. It's vicious in its sensuality. And it works.

"Oh my god…ahhh. I'm gonna…"

I come, and it is massive. She stays onboard. I keep waiting for her to pull off of me.

But she doesn't.

And it makes me feel bad.

And wonderful.

She leans over me.

I think she's gonna grab a sip of my water.

But she spits into it.

"My, that was quite a mouthful, love. You must be all relaxed?"

"I am. Thank you?"

"Sorry aboutchya watah. That was more protein than a girl needs in a day. Thought I might asphyxiate."

"Sorry? I was trying to tell you…"

She gets up and heads to her bathroom.

"Gonna re-brush mah teeth. Mind if I let you sort that out?"

She points to my semen/water milkshake.

Potential little baby Georgies, already expressing their love for the water.

# 11

Some distinct sounds occur in our lives. One of them is a woman getting ready in the morning and trying to be quiet. My dozing back to sleep is punctuated by the *click, clack* of glass makeup jars tapping the countertop. I can hear the silence she creates, in between applications, reviewing her work. Waking up to it soothes me, especially since I don't have to do it myself.

I've been here for over a week, and I still have no idea what Suzanne does. It's some artsy meets corporate thing. Her computer has every type of graphic design software known to man. But she still prefers going old school—a pen and the closest piece of paper. She has more formal pieces, too. Many in frames throughout the house. But her job? It's on the backburner. Where every job should be.

I'm envious of her separation between work and state.

*Click, clack.*

She's almost done.

My girlfriend of ten days kisses me softly on the temple and exits.

If I had to choose which one of my girlfriends was pregnant, I'd choose…

•

"Georgie!"

"You drove the Moke! That makes me so happy!"

"She needs her pistons cleaned. Nice weathah. Thought we'd take her fah a spin."

"The boards on top make it look like an ant carrying two almonds. You're going surfing?"

"We are going surfing. Togethah. An hour's drive. South along the coast. We've gotta wait fah that bloody twat to put down a few stiff ones, before we sink our teeth into him. A little aftah dark."

"We're on our way to a direct confrontation with a violent rapist, and you're throwing in a boys' surf trip."

"Yeah? Thought we'd have a bit of a tribute to my brothah. You game to have a surf?"

"Sure. OK. I'm just not a huge surfer."

"You bloody swim three thousand metahs every othah day. A bit of Styrofoam shouldn't inhibit you too much."

"Cool. OK. I'm down. It's a good idea. PJ would love it. And the Moke strapped with longboards looks fantastic."

"Good. To be honest, couldn't sleep a wink last night. Absolutely dreading this. Thought a paddle might calm the nerves."

Craigo gets anxious before a fight. Who knew? I think this is the most vulnerable I've ever seen him.

"Totally. Me too." I defuse. "I made coffee. You are cream no sugar, right? Want anything else?"

"Yeah, perfect. Grab us a bottle of watah, ay? And make sure you've got yah earphones."

"I do. They're always in my bag. Why?

"The cicadas. They'll make you deaf. Literally."

"Cicadas? Like grasshoppers?"

"Yeah. Trust me. You'll want 'em."

"OK, cool."

"Giddy up!"

Now I know where PJ got *Giddy up!* from.

With the boards rigged on top of the roll bars, there's even more stuff to grab onto, and I go back to my ape hanger posture. If a white sheet flew over me, I'd look like a cartoon ghost.

Moked? Stoked.

•

We pull into the parking lot. It's a stunner. Hills meet the ocean. A simple, yet tasteful bathroom, showers and a food stand. In 'Merica, this would be disgusting, with salt-water taffy and Atlantic City kitsch.

Craigo unties the boards, and I put on sunblock. Families are slowly trekking toward us, heading home.

"This worked out pahfect. Clean, small waves. A little drizzle. Shrinking crowd."

"Yeah, it feels great to cool down a little. Are you gonna call me a poof, if I ask you to put sunblock on my back?"

"I will do no such thing. And I brought you a rashguard, anyway. Solves that."

He points to the big lockbox in the back of the Moke. I open it up, find the rash guard, pull his out and drop my bag in.

"Let's get in the watah!"

He snaps a padlock on the box, and we head across the lot.

"You know I am terrible, right?"

"But paddling is the hardest part. And surely you've got that sorted, ay?"

"True."

"It'll be nice to just get wet. No need to worry about going pro. Plus, that Mal is nice 'n thick. Should be a breeze to get up on." Mal = Malibu = longboard.

PJ had aspirations of going pro. He really was that good. He had the talent. Just maybe not the discipline. Or maybe he just loved to surf more than he loved to compete.

There's no question who his coach was—Craigo. Beer belly aside, the guy has incredible grace. He does all the time, but it shines in the water. Before we've even finished paddling out, he's caught two little waves and walked the board like a tango dancer. Even the goofy stuff he does looks cool—a Quasimodo crouch, petting the water inside the curl.

I need to learn to surf.

Maybe TR will consider it a life skill and let me do a piece?

"You are unbelievable."

"Ay?"

"You look like you came straight out of the womb onto a wave."

"Thanks, mate. Hard not to, growing up here. Let's see you catch a few."

The waves are tiny. I decide to give it a shot. The board he gave me is thick. I could stand up on it, even without a wave.

I go.

Catching it is a breeze.

Push up.

Knees? Wobbly.

Standing up, my butt sticks out like a stinkbug, and my arms flail. What a kook.

"Ahhh!"

A messy fall.

"Georgie! Nice one!"

I rode it for four seconds. Felt like five minutes.

I paddle back out to Craigo.

"That was so rad! I've stood up about a dozen times. But I've never ridden the actual wave like that. Not along the side like how you do. I want another one!"

His broad grin is contagious. Then he effortlessly catches another.

There's this tiny math philosophy book, *Finite and Infinite Games*, by James P. Carse. I found it while burning time in a library. The gist is that there are two types of games: finite games and infinite games. You play finite games to win. You play infinite games to play. The difference between chess and Frisbee. I thought it was thought-provoking at the time. But now? Surfing with Craigo? It makes complete sense. As adults, we're rarely allowed to play. There has to be some goal. Then we age and we return to simplicity. We play. Think of how much more friendly: *Wanna go for a walk?* is compared to: *Wanna arm-wrestle?*

"Do you want me to paddle in and grab your phone? Take a few photos of you surfing for Ava? The ladies love that stuff."

"Nah. She's seen me surf loads of times. Plus, I don't wantchya perving out on my phone, checking out Ava's tits."

"I'd like to think I wouldn't look. But that might be a lie."

"Finally! An undiluted comment about a bird without all yah bloody torment! We'll make you an Aussie yet!"

•

"What time you got?"

"Seven sharp."

We got the dregs at the kiosk at closing time. Two egg salad sandwiches and two bags of chips.

"You gonna finish yah crisps?"

"Go for it." I hand him what remains of my chips. "This is the nicest meal I've ever had before an intervention with a pedophile."

"The pics? What are they? Teenagahs?"

"Worse. I can show you."

"Aftah we eat, please."

"What's the plan?"

"Wait till dark. Scope him out a bit. Then I'll pop in fah a chat. A very frank one. Get the fuck away from my niece, starting this very second. If he resists, I pop out the photos. I'm not sure we want to threaten him with the police. Not tonight."

"Agreed. Keep it simple. How can I help?"

"Nothin'. You hang back. Keep an eye on things. I can imagine he'll get a bit heated. And he won't be ecstatic to have two guys ganging up on him. Especially a sepo."

"Where are you gonna tell him to go? His job's here. His life is fully intertwined with Veronica's. He can't just pick up and move down the street."

"I don't care if he takes a flight tonight to bloody Tassy." Tassy = Tasmania. Craigo tilts his head back and gobbles the last of the chip crumbs.

It really is that simple. Maybe not in a week, when we try to figure out how to prosecute him. But tonight—there's only one task.

I sit on it for a moment.

"Whattaya gonna do about my sistah, Georgie?"

"Uhhh…"

"Look, mate. A bit of a shag on vacation, completely fine. We aren't as prudish here as you are in the States. A root is a root." Root = sex.

"OK?" I'm not sure what he's getting at, but I definitely feel like I'm in trouble.

"Suzanne's track record with the blokes? Terrible. Then nice little Georgie comes along. He's all bringin' her a coffee and listening to her innermost thoughts. Whether you mean to or not, yah're makin' her fall for you. Have you even booked yah flight home yet?"

"Yeah, yeah. I did. Christmas Day."

"Last of the cheap flights?"

"Yeah."

"Maybe a bit of a chat with Suzie, beforehand? She's a big girl. I just don't want her to get hurt."

"Yeah, I know. I know. I'm glad you said that. I've been thinking it. And I hope you don't think my goal in coming out here was…"

"Georgie. We're all good. Just a little bit of eldah brother courtesy. I'm too old to be givin' the old one-two to every bloke that lays eyes on her." He makes a fist.

"Fair enough."

We share half-smiles.

I will miss him.

We watch the ocean mindlessly, like watching a campfire.

The irony of us going to save/protect PJ's unplanned offspring, while I may have one gestating in the oven, is palpable.

•

The little path that shoots off next to the kiosk looks like it's a path to nowhere. Maybe a spot to look at what got caught in the rocks at low tide. But as we go further, I can see that it extends to another beach. A small little cove, with ambient light shining down on it.

"Careful. The drizzle has made these rocks slippery little buggahs."

"Fuck, the cicadas are loud. You weren't kidding."

"Just wait till we get to the cove and up into the canyon. They'll sound like they're takin' ovah."

Craigo stops to watch the last sliver of the sun. Such a romantic. Didn't know he had it in him. He turns over his shoulder toward me.

Then the light catches his arc.

Of urine.

"You might wanna get in on this. Unless you wanna use a dunny up the hill, but they're chock a block full of spidahs."

Sold.

I unzip.

"If only Hitler had hated spiders."

"Amen, brothah."

We're about half way. I can see a boat beached in the little bay.

"That's gotta be Philip Morris's boat, right? I can see the fishing rod holder thingy on the bow. Same as in the photos. From Veronica's house."

"Must be. No one would leave a skiff on the sand, unless they were plannin' on going fishing early in the am."

Now that the sun is gone, it's dark.

Super dark.

We're lucky for the sporadic cloud cover and light drizzle. The reflection gives the slightest tinge of visibility.

I slip in a small tide pool.

"Careful. Just twenty more metahs and we'll be on the grass."

"Wait. One sec."

I stop. Reach into my bag.

"Here."

*Click.*

I turn on his flashlight for him.

"Yah're a legend."

I turn mine on, pleased that I'd set them aside amidst the Ferdinand's garage full of clutter and unfinished craft projects.

The moment the path ends, the sound of the cicadas increases with every step. But the scent of eucalyptus is delicious—a free cough drop in every breath.

The little valley up the hill has a dozen primitive bungalows.

"Jesus."

"Toldja, mate."

"Could this place be any creepier?"

"It's rarely this empty. It's just because of Chrissy."

We both look at one of the two lit bungalows.

With a lit Victoria Bitter neon sign, Philip Morris's crib is not hard to pinpoint.

We spot him in the window, head down in some task.

Fucking nostril flarer.

Craigo leans into my ear. If he shouted from five feet away, I wouldn't' be able to hear him.

It's that loud.

"The printouts? Still dry?"

I pull them from a plastic bag inside my backpack and hand them to him. He flips through a few, clearly trying not to look too hard. He stops on one and points at it.

"That one's just a few years older than Hannah! That mothahfuckah!"

"I know, brother, I know."

Craigo shakes his head in disgust, folds the printouts and slides them into his back pocket.

He's a little casual with our evidence, but it's just before Christmas, and we're wearing shorts, so it feels right. It'd be amazing if he had said, *Why didn't you keep them in a "pedo-file", mate?* But again, we're not here to make quips. We're on a mission.

"Stay here, Georgie. Maybe listen to some music? Shouldn't take more than half an hour."

"Just sit here?"

"Keep an eye on us. Make sure nothing goes pear-shaped."

We watch Philip Morris, fully illuminated in the little surf bungalow. He's engrossed in some hands-on tinkering. And crushing beers. Crushing them. I can see seven empties from here.

"What is he, fucking building a ship in a bottle?"

"Guessing he's adjusting his kit. Maybe making lures."

"Why anyone would make something that costs four dollars?"

"Ay?"

The male cicadas are in charge. And they want some lady cicadas. Really bad.

"Never mind."

I fish out my earphones.

Philip Morris finishes another beer. He's drinking cans. Smart. Because you've gotta lug them all the way in and all the way out of here. Watching him makes me thirsty. But we locked the cooler up in the Moke. Devastating.

Craigo leans in.

"See you in a bit. Stay sharp. He's a bit roasted. If it gets hectic, I may needyah."

I'm envious of how Craigo approaches confronting a guy, at his weird inbred beach home, regarding being a child sex tourist, as not a big deal. Just spectating is giving me a panic attack.

"Wait!"

Craigo looks back at me. Returns.

"Ay?"

"I wanna go. Inside. I wanna go with you." He pauses for a moment.

Craigo acquiesces with his body, then his voice.

"A'right. Suit yahself." He turns back for the door, then back to me. He hands me the printouts. For safekeeping. Ugh. A single drop of pre-rain falls on them, and I slide them into my back pocket. I set my backpack next to the front door, underneath the awning and out of the light drizzle. I stick my earphones on top. I wish I had ten more seconds, to put them away—they cost a small fortune.

The main light on the other cabin up the hill drops. Only a dim little kitchen or bedroom light remains. By comparison, the VB light fixture in Philip's pad makes it look like a closed roadside diner on the way to Vegas.

Craigo knocks.

Through the window, Philip Morris looks annoyed. He has no fear. He walks to the door without hesitation.

"Craigo?"

"G'day, Philip."

"You here at Garie fah the weekend?"

"Just came out fah a surf. Bit hectic in the city."

"You reckon?" Philip Morris cracks a big bro smile. He acknowledges Craigo's appreciation of his favorite spot. I'm sweating my balls off with anxiety. "Can of piss? Just sortin' out the gear."

"Course." Craigo leans over his shoulder, as he walks through the door. He whispers, "All the gear…" Which is slang for *All the gear and no idear*—the guy with all the fancy equipment and no skills. A brilliant, subtle joke.

Philip Morris chucks a beer at me.

Thank god I catch it.

A lob would've sufficed. Clearly, he was pretending it was a grenade.

"Figured you fah soft hands."

"Thanks."

Idiot.

Philip Morris cocks back to chuck one that would take Craigo's head off, and Craigo doesn't even bother to raise his hands.

"Just joking, mate. Here you go." Philip even opens it for him. It fizzes, but not as much as mine is going to.

"Cheers."

"Cheers."

"Cheers. Thanks for the VB."

"You like it?"

"I do."

"Really?"

"Seriously. I even drank a few of yours, when we were babysitting.

I hope that's cool." I wish I was brave enough to not be friendly.

"Course. A bit like Sierra Nevada back in the States, ay?"

"Yeah. Exactly."

Wait. Philip Morris is actually being cool?

"Take a seat, gents. Just kit'in up for tomorrow."

He sits down on one of the two battered couches. We follow and sit opposite. Every second feels like a year.

Philip Morris refocuses on his lures.

Tic…toc.

"Everyone always asks why I make'em mahself. My pop, he said, 'only a poof would rock up and buy…'" Craigo cuts him off.

"Mate, we're not here on a social call."

"Ay?"

He doesn't even look up.

"What's yah plan? With Vee? Char?"

"What is this? A bloody inquisition?"

Now he looks up.

"She's my niece. I have a right to ask."

"Fair 'nough." He pauses for a moment. He's actually thinking about it. This is so fucking weird.

Craigo lets him.

The key to a negotiation is to allow for pauses, and Craigo is no novice. It's tempting to jot down an @AskEsquire.

"A'right. Vee? We get hitched. I adopt Char. Try 'n' get one up the duff fah numbah two. That a'right with you lot?" But he isn't really asking.

Craigo pauses, again. This time for himself. He looks at me. I take a breath, ready to launch into it, but he beats me to the punch.

"No. It's not 'a'right'." Craigo even mimics Philip Morris's meathead drawl on "a'right", which pleases me.

"Ay?"

He sets down the lure and needle nose pliers. It's like the two of them are having this conversation in a well-lit theater, and I'm watching in the pitch-black audience. That's how invisible I am.

"That's not happening, mate."

Uh oh.

"And why not?"

"We've seen the bruises on Vee. Her arms. Her neck. It's time fah you to part ways with my family."

"That bloody twat! What'd she say?!"

"Not word one, Philip, not word one."

Philip Morris starts cracking his knuckles.

Another long pause.

Craigo and Philip Morris stare it down.

"That little cunt! Tell me! Tell me!" Philip flexes his back, taunting Craigo. This highlights two things: Philip Morris is way bigger than Craigo, and based on his lats, he would have made a great swimmer. Or king cobra.

"She didn't have to tell us. She looks like a bloody punching bag." Craigo flexes his back, too. But it's…let's just say it's a little smaller.

They're in a standoff. Philip Morris looks like he's going to throttle Craigo. Their eyes are in a time-warp lock.

Fuck it.

I fish out the printouts from my sweaty back pocket. Unfolding them, they're moist but still intact.

"Philip. That's not the only thing we're concerned about." My voice shakes. I lay the printouts in front of him.

He looks confused, surprised to see me engage.

He picks one up. The topmost one. With him in it. The selfie with his witless grin staring back up at him.

Still holding the printout, his gears start churning. All that combusts is pure fury. He looks at me for a moment, but he hones in on Craigo.

"You mothahfuckahs!" It all comes together for him. He may be an idiot, but he's not dumb.

Craigo is already crouching, sensing the altercation. Philip Morris stands. Philip is massive. His upright torso dims the lights into shadow.

Craigo, smartly, backs toward the door. I am paralyzed.

"YOU THINK YOU CAN COME INTAH MY HOUSE…"

Now, Craigo is standing in the open doorway, about to back-step outside. Philip lunges. He drives into Craigo with his shoulder. The sound is sickening.

"YOU MOTHAH FUUU …"

They roll down the front steps.

Craigo scrambles up, pivots and hits Philip hard in the kidneys. The sound is even more gruesome than Philip's pile drive. It stuns Philip Morris—that Craigo is fighting back. But Craigo is wheezing. Philip knocked every ounce of air out of him.

I step outside and quickly look up the hill at the other inhabited bungalow.

Nothing.

Philip is gasping, and Craigo is recovering, holding his ground. Not advancing, not retreating. A gentleman's fighter. But it's the wrong night to have manners.

Philip's face turns taunted-bull furious, and he swings at Craigo. Again. Craigo is so much shorter than him, Philip swings are diagonal. They're fierce, but they miss. Craigo's head movement is fluid, effortless. With every miss, Philip gets more and more livid.

Craigo lands a couple of surgical body shots.

Philip coughs.

Maybe we can go home soon.

The light drizzle that started when got here has turned to rain.

Philip Morris struts toward Craigo. Craigo holds back for a split second. He goes for an uppercut but loses his footing in the mud, and the slow-motion fist is caught by Philip.

"Fuuuck." (that was me)

Philip pulls him to the ground like a rag doll. Either he watches a lot of MMA or wrestled in high school, because Philip Morris's ground game is strong.

Pin, chokehold. And he's not stopping.

"YOU BLOODY WANK! YOU COME HERE! THREATEN ME!"

Fuck.

I look around for a rock, but it's so dark and wet. Nothing stands out.

"Uuulth, uulth…" Craigo's gasps get stickier, more guttural.

I see my bag. The earphones on top. No other choice.

I yank the cord out of the Beats headphones, take two running steps and jump onto Philip Morris's back.

I wrap the cord around his neck in an instant, and in the time it takes him to react and let go of Craigo, I pull it tight, cross the cord and twist it twice.

"Uuunht!"

Craigo gasps.

I pull tighter.

Philips launches an elbow at my side.

"Agh."

Fuck, he is powerful.

Pulling, pulling. The rope burns on my hands feel like they might ignite. But Philip Morris is so strong. He sits up on his knees as if I am weightless, like an empty backpack. He's twisting, but slowly. Trying to get his fingers underneath the cord. But it's too tight.

"Uuunht." Craigo's second breath. This one sounds less desperate.

Philip gives up on his neck and throws more elbows.

They land. But they're soft. He's fading.

"Ouuughth." The taste of puke hits my mouth, from clenching so tight. But I'm not letting go. If it weren't cinched, I wouldn't be able to hold it.

Craigo comes to my rescue. He hits Philip Morris so many times, so quickly, it looks mechanical. Face, chest, stomach, repeat.

Crack.

Philip's jaw breaks.

Craigo puts another one in motion.

But Philip slumps.

Time stands still. Craigo, missing the now slouching Philip Morris, connects with my eye. I don't blackout, but everything freezes.

Philip is lifeless. I let go. He doesn't move. He's not dead, but his warrior spirit is gone. He's given up, stopped fighting. I release the cords, and they stick to the indentations in my palms.

I dismount him.

He struggles to resurrect his breathing. With the threat gone, Craigo and I catch our breath. My eyes are fixated on Philip Morris's nose. He's back to nostril flaring. He'll be OK.

Craigo's jaw drops open. Just like with Hannah and Zero Dad. Taking in more oxygen. Calming himself.

Wait.

He doesn't look calmer.

No no no…

There's not an ounce of fight left in Philip Morris. Craigo pounces on him, grabbing the Beats cords where they lay. Pulls them. Much harder than I could have.

"No no no no no!"

But I'm inaudible to Craigo. The cicadas are thunderous.

And he keeps pulling. And pulling.

"Craigo! Let go! Let him go!"

"Guurghhh." Philips' mouth is dry, and no air is moving. He drops, piece by piece to the ground. Craigo is still hanging on him, like a battered price tag.

"Craigo! You're gonna kiiilll…"

If you tried to cut a cantaloupe with a guitar string. That's what it looks like. The skin resists and resists. And then, finally, it lets go. The moment Philip Morris's throat muscles pause, Craigo's taut pull severs his neck. Blood.

So much blood.

His life ends, after four disgusting coughs.

"Fuuuck!"

Craigo stumbles back in shock. He untangles himself to avoid the pouring of blood.

"You fucking killed him!"

Craigo looks like he feels nothing.

I look down at the earphone cord marks on my hands.

"Craigo, it was over! Why?" He can't hear me. The soundtrack of cicadas is deafening. He leans down toward me.

"Bloody hell, that's a lotta blood, ay?"

"Are you fucking crazy? You just killed a guy!"

"Mate, it had to be done."

"He's a cop! We're fucked!"

"I couldn't give a shit. That fuckah's dead. We came here with a problem. That problem is fixed. Now, we just have a slightly different problem."

"Are you out of your mind?"

So much blood.

Small rivers of rain and blood trickle downhill.

Craigo starts pacing.

I do a quick scan of our status. Still no one around. No response from the bungalow up the hill. We're in near complete darkness. The only ambient lights are the dim light from the other bungalow and the illumination of the Victoria Bitter neon. Our two greatest risks are: 1. wandering lovers looking to escape the city, and 2. the other bungalow's occupants going on a moonlit stroll. Both scenarios are unlikely, given the rain.

The seconds creep by. My mind wanders.

*@stopdropnroll My girlfriend treats me so terribly, I could murder her sometimes. How do I control the anger?*

*@AskEsquire Hide the body. Erase the crime scene.*

OK.

Think.

Relax.

Think.

Think.

"Want a beer?"

"AY?"

"Our DNA is already all over Philip's house. You are covered in blood. I am not. We need to chill and assess." I don't wait for him to weigh in. "I'm gonna go back inside and cut all of the lights but that one." I point to the VB neon sign.

Don't let anyone tell you that beer advertising doesn't work.

# 12

The inside of the house didn't really look too bad. Maybe the plan I'm formulating on the fly will work. I set four beers in between us.

Craigo nods. He catches his own reflection in the window.

"I look like a tampon stuck undahneath a gumboot."

"And he's back. My eye is killing me. Thanks a lot 'mate'."

"It was gettin' a bit upside down. I might've come in a bit hot. Apologies."

"A bit hot? Holy understatement. But you don't have to say you're sorry. Honestly, I'll only be sorry if we go to jail. Fuck that motherfucker."

"Cheers to that. Good riddance."

Philip Morris could not look deader.

Craigo slouches.

Drops his forearms on his knees.

He's done.

Nothing left in the tank.

"OK. I think I've got a plan."

"Ay?"

I motion him closer. The fucking cicadas. But they may have helped us.

"I SAID I THINK I'VE GOT A PLAN."

"Stop yelling, mate, I'm only five centimetahs from you."

"Sorry, I got concert voice for a sec. OK. Check it out. How many empty beers in the house?"

"Ten? Maybe more. He hits the piss pretty hard. Don't think he'd've tackled me, if he wasn't off his rockah."

"Good."

I pound my beer and open another.

Craigo follows.

"There's a reservoir on top of the dunny. We need to get the blood off of us. Mostly you. The rain is to our advantage, as it'll make most of this pretty murky. Go in the dunny. It looks like it might have a shower?"

"Yeah?"

"Take a shower. Get the cleanest you've ever been in your life. Clothes, too. I'll go back inside, make sure nothing seems too weird."

"OK."

"I'm gonna turn off the VB light, and leave something on in the back of the house, like the bedroom light. Just enough light so we can see but dark enough so that no one can see us. We're gonna make it look like he went drunk fishing, got caught on his lines and drowned."

"That is idiotic."

"It will work. We fully admit to having a conversation with him. We make sure we get back to Bondi as soon as possible. Buy some stuff. Get a receipt from a gas station. They'll find Philip Morris in a few days, with fuck loads of sea life living in his carcass, at the bottom of that bay. A few VBs in the skiff, ten here. It's believable. The rain is our friend. Right now? Our best friend."

"Yeah? Until we say why we were here. And we tell the coppah's what?"

"The truth. That he beat Veronica. That he was a pedophile. We get them to check his computer." He's starting to buy it. "You think law enforcement leadership wants to spend ten fucking minutes trying to find a perpetrator for killing a bad cop? A woman beating pedophile rapist? We're doing them a favor."

"Didju have this in mind before we came, Georgie?"

"Absolutely not. But right now, we're fucked."

"I fucked us. I'm so sorry, mate."

"We'll be OK. Let's start moving. Hit the shower. And remember, not one drop of blood. Anywhere."

I look down at dead Philip Morris.

Fuck him.

Craigo stands up and walks to the dunny.

Even pretending to be hyper-competent calms me. I walk back into the house, open two more beers and pour them out. Leaving them as more damning evidence. One of them, I pour a little more into my mouth than the sink.

•

My plan is coming together. The house is as innocuous as possible. I put spare clothes for each of us into plastic bags and chuck a bunch of Philip Morris's fishing gear into another.

Craigo emerges from the shower. He's mumbling something, but I can't hear him. The cicadas. But I can smell him—fresh as a daisy.

"Did you use an entire bar of soap?" He holds up two fingers. He grabs the bag of clothes I left next to the dunny, dresses quickly and sits down next to me. I hand him my current beer, and he takes a sip while looking at Philip Morris.

"Christ. Whattah debacle."

"Craigo. I've got it. Just stay with me. OK?"

"It's yah show. Hope they'll give us adjoining cells. And conjugal visits."

He cracks the slightest smile. We make a great team. Briefly, I'm tempted to alert him that our conjugal visits would involve his sister visiting me. But I'm not sure if this joke would ever be funny.

I roll Philip onto his side. Even though most of the blood has coagulated, it gets all over me. I keep wiping my hands, to try to keep the blood off of the rest of Philip's clothes.

Now, with only the back bedroom light on, it's really hard to see. Craigo rubs his hands. His must be even more inflamed than mine. I need to send an email to Dr. Dre and ask that they try a different material for their multipurpose earphone cords.

Craigo pulls out his flashlight.

"Hey! No flashlights until we really need them. OK?"

"Gotchya."

"Have you seen a boat dolly?"

"Yeah, the neighbahs have one."

"Is there a boat on it?"

"'Course. What the hell else is gonna be on it?"

"We need an empty one. Can you grab Philip's from the beach?"

"What am I? Yah bloody secretary?"

"I'm fucking covered in blood, yo!"

"A'right, a'right."

I shrug.

He returns with the dolly.

"Perfect."

"Ay?"

"Nothing. OK. Stop right there. The dunny. Was there a shower curtain?"

"Yeah?"

"Grab it." Why you would keep your archaic outhouse and add full plumbing and a shower to it, versus add it to the cabin, is beyond me. But that's how it works here.

Craigo looks slightly fed up with taking orders, but every time he considers protesting, he looks at my t-shirt and stops. It couldn't be more bloody if you printed *massacre* on it.

He complies.

"OK. Listen but don't touch me. I'm gonna wheel this dead piece of garbage to the water. Dunk myself. Leave my wet clothes on the sand."

"But yah're already soaking."

"Yeah, but I'm soaking in blood. And that's what we need to worry about. I'll get him down there, clean everything as well as possible and take him out."

He's not getting it.

"So…I?"

"All you have to do is minimize the remaining crime scene here. Pour that entire reservoir over this front area. Make it a wet swampland. No blood equals no crime scene. Then grab my bloody clothes and the shower curtain from the beach and meet me back at the parking lot. Try to keep the spare clothes I stole from Philip's house clean and dry—obviously separate from any blood."

"Christ Georgie, I've got it. But whattaya gonna do?"

"I'm gonna strip down, weigh him down, wrap him in fishing line and feed him to the fish."

"But the boat? It'll be a dead giveaway?"

"I won't be in the fucking boat."

Does he really not get it?

"But how are you…"

"I'm gonna swim. Straight over and across to you."

"You've got tah be keeeding me?"

"I'm not. What the fuck else are we gonna do? Look at his neck. If we don't give the fishies a shot at erasing that, it's gonna look like someone took a bandsaw to him."

"Christ."

"Just stay as clean as possible, OK? Dilute his blood with water from the dunny. Use that bucket. There's a spout next to the door of the dunny. We don't have to erase that we were here, just that we committed a crime here."

"Why are you so bloody calm?"

"I have no idea. Just clean up. And stay clean. And keep my clean clothes separate from these." I point my thumb up to my bloody t-shirt. "I'll rinse them in the water, but they'll still have a ton of blood on them."

"What about the sharks? They're no joke."

"I thought all of the beaches were netted?"

"Yeah, in Sydney! At the kiddie beaches! There are miles and miles of beach here, mate."

"It's OK. We don't have a choice." I look up at the other bungalow. "And keep a vigilant eye on the other bungalow. If you see ANY more light coming from it, flash your flashlight out at the water three times. Just do something to alert me. Worst case is we'll play drunk, that we came here to surf and fish and to fuck around. With our good buddy Philip Morris." We look down at him.

Still dead.

"A'right. Giddy up."

"Don't leave anything behind on the beach, besides the boat dolly."

He heads for the bucket next to the dunny, and I roll up Philip Morris in the shower curtain. Everything is wet and muddy; it's like gift wrapping a bag of spaghetti. But no one is complaining about the rain right now. What a godsend.

I flip him onto his back. The darkness, the blood, the mud, the cicadas. Craigo choked this fucker to death. And my headphone cords are stuck in his neck.

I pull the cord out and set it next to the tackle box, pointing it out to Craigo as he begins to clean. He nods. The blood around Philip's neck is syrupy, and pulling the cord out releases a burp of blood. It's so visceral. I suppress it for a future nightmare. There will be many.

He's lost a lot of blood, but he's still damn heavy.

"Dead weight. You motherfucker."

"Ay?"

Craigo leans down to help me pick him up.

"No! Stop! Stay clean, OK?" But it was nice he offered to help.

"Right, right."

"But thanks for offering."

He shakes his head at my odd-timed pleasantry.

I push the contraption ten feet.

Dead Philip Morris really likes to slither off the boat dolly. But the shower curtain keeps him contained. I'm able to keep him crammed into economy seating.

Off we go.

I nod to Craigo.

The singularity of my purpose calms me.

We make it to the beach without incident.

I get him next to the boat, take a breath and stealthily slide into the water. Maybe I've seen too many CSI episodes, but blood is the enemy.

The sound of the cicadas has faded. It's been replaced by small, crumbling waves. Heavenly.

Craigo pops out of nowhere.

"Fuck, Craigo! You scared me to death!"

He's got the tackle box, fishing pole, fishing lure vest, four empty VBs and two full ones. I can see he's got the rest of the beers in a plastic bag. He's already double-checked the house. Good boy.

He looks at the tackle box, opens it and points at the printouts.

"A criminal mastahmind yah not, Georgie."

"Hey! I'm not saying I forgot the printouts. But I'm not saying I didn't." We laugh at how fucked we are. "And we don't have time for a beer. I need to get out there."

"One to pour all ovah the boat and tackle box. The othah is fah you. You'll need it. Careful of yah fingahprints. See you on the othah side. Wrap yah clothes, the bloody headphone cord, earphones and the showah curtain up, tight. Pop 'em in the plastic bag. I'll sort them out."

His confidence is back. I nod.

"Game time."

"Yep. Tight lines."

He gives a forced half-smile. I can tell that he's worried for me.

The boat has an inch of water in it from the rain. I bilge it out with a Tupperware bowl that was clearly left for this purpose. With one big grunt, I flop curtain-wrapped Philip Morris into the boat.

I slide him to the front of the boat, lean his bloody head off the front and slide the curtain off of him—trying to minimize the blood touching the boat. It's not perfect, but it works well enough.

Craigo, knowing he can't help, stands back a bit, in the shadows.

Watching me. Waiting for his job to start.

In between each step, I dunk myself and whatever I've touched in the water—slowly shrinking the blood trail.

The shower curtain will be a nightmare to attempt to clean, but when aren't they? I do wonder if a missing shower curtain in the dunny will look suspicious. But getting it clean enough to put it back is not an option. It's one of the many flaws of my plan. But as in life, some risk is unavoidable.

The only thing that really breaks me is the boat dolly. The blood loves to stick to it, and even using my own shirt doesn't work. As a last resort, I take it in the ocean with me. It's like going for a dip with a weight bench. Exfoliating it with some sand, it finally shines.

I pull my wet sand trick on the shower curtain. It works. I roll it up and hand it to Craigo.

"Christ."

He nods with approval, while stuffing it in the evidence-filled plastic bag. What he will do with it, I have no idea. A problem for another time.

He heads back up the hill, presumably to do one last walk through and kill the lights. I hope he takes his time, because I need that light.

Wearing Philip Morris's clean clothes, he looks like a bald little boy wearing his dad's shirt.

It's time to shove us off.

It's outgoing tide, and I'm thankful. I need the rest. The water pulls us slowly, steadily. It grows eerily quiet, as our distance from the shore increases.

The boat has a little outboard and oars. I opt for a single oar and take us. I've gotta reach the end of the bay but not much further. If I go too far, I risk getting pulled out by the tide and/or getting lost and/or drowning. And only one of us is drowning tonight.

Full of lures and weights, the fishing vest is nice and heavy. I roll Philip's ugly ass over and put it on him. It's an oddly intimate gesture.

His expression has lost its resting dickhead face. It's almost serene.

I pop the beers and cheers him. His final rites.

"May you rest in peace, you piece of fucking shit."

I yank some fishing line out.

*Zeee.*

I find his heaviest lure, tie it to the line and wrap it around his neck. His strangled throat catches the line perfectly. I hook the lure in the toe of his shoe, like a clumsy mis-cast.

A dozen beers and a casting gone awry. I can't tell whether this is ridiculous or simple and good. Hopefully the latter.

It's hard getting him to the edge, but once I roll him into the water, he doesn't so much as float as he does pause. Then? He sinks like a wet sack of laundry.

You don't need a lot of weight to sink a human. Just enough to offset the remaining air in their lungs and their blood. Jump in a pool with a few rolls of quarters sometime, and you'll see what I mean.

*Zeeet…zee zee zeet.*

I keep the fishing pole under my foot.

He sinks further than I expected.

A good thing.

I wipe the rod against my underwear, smudging any chance of a fingerprint and chuck it in the water.

I was planning on leaving the pole stuck in the boat, using Philip Morris as our anchor. But the boat will drift, and he will not. And the harder it is to find him, the more fish will have eaten away at his neck meat. A bit disgusting, but also pragmatic.

So far, the two lit bungalows have allowed me to triangulate my position and progress. I can even make out the faint light of Philip Morris's pad flickering, as Craigo does his last sweep.

*Click.*

The light in the upper bungalow just disappeared.

Bedtime.

Sure, it's good news. They're probably old. Have had this inholding for decades. No cable out here. Read a few pages of a thriller and went to bed. And they won't be witnesses at our murder trial.

But now, I only have the dim light from the back bedroom of the house, my sense of direction and the stars. And it's cloudy.

Time to clean up my crime scene.

A sip of beer.

Tupperware.

Pour pour pour.

Scoop scoop scoop.

Wipe wipe wipe.

Repeat.

In my soaking wet boxer briefs, my shrunken balls clinging together for warmth, I must look like an idiot.

I clean off the Tupperware, VB cans and tackle box. The good news is that any teeny drop of blood I might have missed will be Philip Morris's. Cleaning the tackle box requires me to pull off my boxer briefs and use them as a rag. Of all of the days not to wear a Speedo…

The cleaning and bilging process has worked. Enough. It's time to go.

I slide my wet crumpled boxer briefs back on.

Awful.

*Blubby blubbity blub blub.*

Philip Morris's body has off-gassed.

Disgusting.

•

I slide into the water, minimizing my disturbance. Craigo's warning about sharks is no joke, and I subtly sidestroke away from the boat. The cool water soothes my rope-burnt hands.

Philip Morris's house goes dark.

Craigo's done and heading to the Moke.

Pitch black.

I was hoping I had another ten minutes of orientation, to make some progress. A trained swimmer can swim about half as fast as a slow walker. On flat ground, you could walk three to four miles an hour. In a pool, I can swim two miles an hour. Maybe a little faster. Add hills to the walker or an open body of water to the swimmer and both speeds get cut in half. I've got roughly a mile's swim. With the current, it'll take an hour. A tough, tough hour.

The boat's about a hundred feet away, and based on our drifting, his body is even further. There's movement in the water underneath me. A school of fish? A big fish about to teach school? I take solace in the fact that Philip Morris's big meaty body and open wounds are a lot more enticing to a predator than my skinny ass. Regardless, there's nothing I can do. But damn, the sidestroke is slow.

To be a certified Red Cross swim instructor, you have to master all of the strokes. And you get taught some bonus ones, too—like how to tread water for two days if you're lost at sea. To minimize the splashing and turbulence, both for sharks and anyone that could possibly catch my silhouette, I transition to a modified combat stroke. It's sidestroke meets the breast stroke meets freestyle. It's what they teach Navy Seals for efficiency and stealth. It's not as fast as freestyle, but it keeps my hands from exiting the water. Less splashing. Less eye catching. The right call. But I suck at it.

A few more minutes and I can barely see the boat. It's far enough away now. In one movement, I transition to freestyle. Opening up the fuel lines. Speeding up feels good.

Stroke stroke stroke…breathe.

Stroke stroke stroke…breathe.

Every ten breaths, I stop and re-orient myself. The clouds have broken a little, and there's a slight reflection on the water. I can make out the rolling hills. And I have to presume the dark spot way up ahead is the lightless parking lot.

Way up ahead.

I just helped kill a guy and dump his body. So many decisions. So many opportunities for mistakes. It feels good to move. To do something I'm good at. It's mechanical. And thoughtless.

I stop. Breathe. Look around.

More cloud clearing.

Complete blackness. Stars. Entire constellations.

But they're even more disorienting.

I look back to the shore.

Nothing.

Wait.

What is that?

Some reflection?

I wait.

I swim sidestroke with my head above water and keep my eyes where I saw the glimmer.

Bink.

I start counting.

1, 2, 3…

More sidestroke. I close my left eye, to see it better. But it's already half-closed. Swollen from Craigo's fist.

34, 35, 36…

Bink.

Something is strobing on the beach.

A beachgoer's cellphone?

Craigo?

It is vaguely on my route. But it's so dark. I look behind me. Up. Catch my breath. I pause and look through a large cloud clearing, right before turning to stroke. There it is. The Southern Cross. It's behind me. Indicating south.

Not exactly behind me, but it's good enough. I'm supposed to be heading north, and I am. It's a bit obvious, but it still comforts me.

I'm on my way.

Stroke stroke stroke…breathe…look.

•

Boxer briefs clinging to what remains of my penis that has not retracted into my abdomen, Craigo yanks me into a hug and slaps my back with a towel. It's a pretty intimate move for an Aussie. I can tell that the waiting stressed him out.

"That beacon thing you did saved me. Saved me."

"Thank god you could see it. I was so busy trying to hide it, all tucked behind the towel. Glad you had yah smarts on high alert."

I nod and try to catch my breath.

"It was a propah swim, ay? I had faith in you, Georgie, but it's a long ways."

The shivering starts.

"Clothes in the Moke. Didn't want to get 'em too sandy. You sure look clean."

"Salt water cures all."

"Sorry 'bout the eye."

We walk back to the car. I dry off. There's only one other car in the parking lot, and it's got old people stickers. *Public Radio, Hang Up & Drive*, etc.—must belong to our neighbors up the hill. An ageist is something that I am not. But if there's a trial and I have to badmouth their vision and hearing to keep from going to prison and getting raped? Blind old fuckers they will be.

Ancient clothes await me on the passenger seat of the Moke. They must've been Philip Morris's dad's, because they're only a little big. And they smell old. Like an old man. A flannel shirt so worn out, it doesn't have enough stamina to wrinkle. But it's dry, takes the chill off and doesn't look so absurd as to spark attention if we get stopped on the way home.

"Pop this on, mate. And keep yah head down. It's dark, but we don't need anyone seein' yah shinah." He hands me one of Philip Morris's baseball hats: *Deep Sea Fishing Charters, Sydney.*

"Classic."

Nestling into the Moke, my head falls back. It's the first moment I've not had a single thing to do, since I began my life of crime. The longboard bag on the rack has a slight bulge, and I figure that's where Craigo stashed our bloody contraband.

Smart.

Super smart.

I can't wait to get out of this creepy dark parking lot. And neither can Craigo. Vroom Vroom.

Winding back onto the main roads, it does feel like we're running. Like we're criminals and flashing lights are going to creep up behind us at any moment. But they don't. Regardless, every car that passes by us going the other way makes me hold my breath.

Turns. More winding. Civilization slowly returns, with the scattered houses becoming more frequent.

We get out to a four-laner, closer to Sydney, and stop at a

crosswalk. Some broey guy passes by the Moke and nods in appreciation. Craigo acknowledges.

Maybe everything is going to be OK?

Still, I'm so wound up. I need a Xanax or to get something off my…

"Shawna might be pregnant. She's late."

"Ay?"

"My old girlfriend. She came out to Panama about six weeks ago."

"Why the FUCK are you tellin' me this right now?"

"I dunno, I just…"

"Does my sistah know?" He looks over at me. I try to return his gaze, but my left eye is now fully glazed over, making everything blurry.

"Uhhh…"

"Nevah mind. I already know the answah." He grips the steering wheel, staring ahead. "Christ mate. Does it evah end? Have you not learned anything from my brothah?"

"I'm sorry. I just can't deal with all the secrecy."

"Bloody hell." He shakes his head and shifts through the gears. "Yah're only here a few more days. Tell Suzanne once yah're home fah a few weeks. Not soonah. And goddamnit mate, not one word to her about tonight, a'right?"

"OK."

"Here's the plan. We went out to see Philip. Had a bit of a chat. He was a twat. On the piss, loaded. Told us to fuck off. We grabbed a sunset surf, chilled on the sand for a few and came home. We show our faces. Pop in around Bondi. Create a papah trail. No one's the wiser."

"Agreed. But I was thinking. No one even knew we were there."

"False. Veronica knew we were going. My sistah nearly gave us a send-off. The Garie Beach parking cops likely have our plate or could match it with the parking receipt. Plus, anyone who looked hard enough would see us on one of a dozen traffic cameras on the way."

He's right.

"Yeah, but Suza…"

"My sistah is a lush, mate. She shacks up with married guys. Callin' em up late, aftah a bottle of wine. I love her. I trust her. But cannot bet our lives on her being able to keep a secret. It's a low risk, but it's not zero."

"Yeah, yeah. OK. I'd rather not rehash it anyway."

He nods in agreement and pulls into a Bondi Caltex station, even though we don't need gas. He stops next to the glass front door, and the attendant nods with approval at the Moke. You just can't lose with this ride.

"Stay here. And keep yah head down."

"Maybe some chips or nuts or…"

Craigo shakes his head at my petty request.

He returns with four bags of chips and two massive off-brand hydration drinks.

"Oh my god. I love you. I forgot how much swimming makes me…"

"Eatchya crisps. This wasn't a pleasure stop."

He throws two bags at me, and one nicks my forehead.

"Watch the eye, dick."

But he's busy fiddling with the side mirror, as we slowly pull away.

The rain returns, faster than our crawl.

I pop my head back to the front of the store and see it. Security camera. Craigo is documenting us. Getting the extremely unsubtle orange Moke on camera. From the angle we drove away, he must've dropped the license plate in the dead center of the camera for a solid two seconds. I know I am a major participant in this plan, but intentionally documenting us makes me feel like a real criminal. And I can't help but wonder if the camera caught more than his license plate. My finger unintentionally drags across the bulge in the surfboard bag overhead—replete with felony-convicting DNA.

Premeditated murder makes so much more sense now. An invisible rented sedan from Hertz is a far better murder machine than a charming pumpkin of a convertible that begs for a glance and a smile.

Raindrops hit Craigo's head, as he shifts the gears of the Moke. He gingerly pulls the Caltex receipt out from his pocket and hands it to me, palm down, shielding it from the rain. I pull the plastic shopping bag out of my bag. The one that kept the evidence intact.

I grab the receipt and wrap it in the bag. Craigo nods. I want to acknowledge our epic teamwork. But a high five seems inappropriate.

Full rain downpour. The surfboard roof creates sheets of water, like rusted out rain gutters.

Moked? Soaked.

# 13

"Pop the boards inside, ay? I'm gonna get her dry, before I slide her indoors."

"Gotcha."

I point to the ashtray, where I stuck the Caltex and Garie Beach parking receipts, wrapped in the plastic bag. They're the only dry items within ten feet.

"Yeah, grab 'em. Protect 'em with yah life. Snag some new clothes, too. You look like a creepy wet old geezah."

•

*Your honor. The jury. I'd like to present evidence numbers A1 and A2. A Caltex receipt showing pretzels…* My head chews on incarceration, as I lay the receipts out on Craigo's desk. I grab a refrigerator magnet to protect them and weigh them down. The magnet is a thick, naked woman, flashing a big smile while steering a Vespa.

I stack up one of the surfboards in the corner and lay the other on the ground. The evidence one.

I unpack it.

The salt water did a better job than I'd have guessed. And Craigo had the shower curtain, earphones, cord and wet clothes wrapped so tight, his surfboard is completely clean. Still, I strip off Philip Morris Senior's flannel and wipe the board down, before leaning it back up against the other one.

It seems like a year has passed since I was choking him. But seeing the bloody earphone cord brings it all back. I can still feel it digging into my hands.

By the time Craigo arrives, I'm down to my skivvies, with the old flannel and grandpa utility shorts rounding out the pile.

"You've not changed yet, ay?"

"I'm trying to tighten it up. Board is spotless. Clothes are in that bag."

"Good. Good. Pop us a bottle of piss?"

"Done. Was just thinking the same thing. It's sweet to have a retail shop. I mean, if you were a serial murderer? Come on. I just grabbed a towel off the rack and stuck the whole thing in a We've Gotchya Back bag from the register. So convenient. But how are we gonna…"

"Whattaya on about?"

I point to the ball of evidence. I wrapped it one additional time, with an Aussie flag towel from the shop. It looks like a weakly wrapped housewarming gift for Australia Day—their version of the 4th of July.

He nods.

"She'll be right. Lemme work."

"OK. Sorry."

I look at the beach towel travesty and stay quiet.

"Go. And grab anothah hat, you wank."

He yanks Philip's baseball hat off my head and throws it on the pile. I just realized that I'd been in my underwear and his hat, hanging out in the office.

Nice job, Georgie.

Craigo has done a fine job of elevating his shop with original decor and quippy apparel, but the aisles of WGB will never be mistaken for Urban Outfitters.

The duplicate staffer WGB t-shirt feels both unclever and just right. And it fits.

A pair of sale-rack board shorts hang off my boney hips, and I return to Craigo.

"One of the staffah shirts? Not what I would've chosen but good. Memorable." He grabs a WGB hat from his desk. "Let's pop this on, to seal the deal."

Fitting the hat to my head, the fluorescent lights catch my face, and Craigo takes notice.

"Did I hitchya that hard, Georgie? Thought I'd limp wristed it."

"Yeah, you diii…"

But again, he's not listening. He's at the edge of the shop, rifling through the bone yard of discarded t-shirt mistakes, silkscreen ink and endless bottles of chemicals. All of the necessary evils to keep our fashion sense up to date. Like the one currently being silkscreened—

*Interracial dating goes together like white on rice*—a must-have. OSHA would love to peruse this corner.

Briefly, I think of the phrase you hear in every store: *Do you have any more in the back?* The back is a fake place. Your hidden treasure in the perfect size is not here. Inventory is the front. The back is not a magical Narnia. It's where work gets done. Where the sausage gets made.

Craigo manhandles a fifty-five gallon drum. How much is fifty-five gallons in kilos? I can't do it; my head hurts too much. He pops the cover and jumps back. The smell reaches me, twenty feet away.

It smells like liquid rat poison mixed with paint thinner.

The chemicals make my good eye water.

He grabs a one-gallon tin with more warnings than a Tupac album cover and pours it in.

Next, our pile of evidence goes in.

God I hope I'm not here when he pulls that stuff out.

So toxic.

Guilt management—I pop him a beer.

"You sorted fah a bendah, mate?"

"Huh?" If I'm not looking directly at Craigo when he talks, I lose most of what he says.

He looks at me for one second. Like he's going to share a secret. But he stops and keeps it to himself.

I'm glad. I'm all secreted out.

"I'm still formulating our alibi, but one thing's fah certain—we've got to go get good and pissed. Just solidifies our inability to be part of any capah."

"I'm working on it."

One more beer. Gone.

"Good. Drink at least two more, and meet me at Ravesis. A'right?"

"Drink by myself and then meet you at a 'Yank' bar? Why? We just fucking executed…"

"Mate, just bloody do it."

He stares me down. For a moment today, I thought I was briefly in charge. At least of my life. At least of being a proactive person. But even after hiding a dead body with my own hands, I'm not. I still feel like a fuck up.

A follower. A passenger.

"OK. OK." I fully acquiesce. "Why there? The other bars…"

"Because it's a Yank bar. Enough. Drink yahself silly fah twenty minutes. Meet me. No mattah what happens, do not say a word. You a'right?"

"Yeah, I'm cool."

"See you in a bit. Giddy up."

I do not challenge him. Even though all I want to do is walk up the hill and cross over into quiet Bronte. What I would do to be fumbling with the lock on the back sliding glass door, walking in and laying down to fall asleep. Especially with my head in Suzanne's lap.

•

I've taken several long pees since downing the liter of electrolyte juice from the Caltex station. I'm four beers deep since Craigo left. In the week plus that we've been working together, Craigo's beer supply has been tapped, and our empties look like a mismatched glass platoon: thirty Coopers, a Carlton Cold, two Tooheys and a single VB stubbie bottle.

Philip Morris would be proud.

•

With one more beer and nineteen more minutes to kill, my mind wanders back to Suzanne. Then to Shawna.

My own love life + restlessness = I log into my Twitter queue on Craigo's iMac.

*@indoorsy i'm in a love triangle. i love them both. how do i pick one?*

*@AskEsquire Pick the one you love. If you love them both, you have to walk away from both.*

One of the reasons that PJ's parents settled in Bronte was because Bondi was just too much. Think of living in Venice Beach. Magic, right? Then, one summer after another drunk fool urinates on your porch, you get the option to cash out and move to Pacific Palisades. The same salty air, wide-open view of the ocean. Minus the noise, minus the pointless vandalism.

The goal of life: unlimited access, with limited crowds.

Us versus them.

As I continue to get wasted, I rethink writing TR an email and continue spiraling down this topic. The separation between the rich and the poor. The chasm between anyone and someone else. Aussies and Yanks. Cops and civilians. Anyone who is not us.

When I bore myself, I know I'm drunk.

How many beers is that?

Time to go to Ravesis.

And get our timestamp. And be documented. And be seen.

•

Growing up in Southern California, you can't escape the military. The Navy in Coronado. The Marines in Camp Pendleton. The pristinely located ocean-side Air Force bases like Vandenburg.

The Recon Marines on the news talk about being adrenaline drunk. Not those exact words, but there is a sensation of having your senses so heavily overloaded that you struggle to recover at the time and sometimes never fully recover after. It's a stepping stone to PTSD.

And that's how I feel.

I've got a certified Red Cross Swim Instructor card in my wallet, a growing black eye, fear of fatherhood, incarceration and prison rape, the patriotism of a man abroad and the buzz of a too long of a swim rehydrated with a beer sampler pack.

With such cohesive tools, what could go wrong?

I walk the block to Ravesis.

The bouncer is busy chatting up a group of young females and doesn't notice that I should be walking away from a bar, not into one. Ten seconds pass. I'm starting to think that this was a bad, bad idea. The crowd. The sounds of NFL highlights combined with cricket highlights on the smaller TV. Aussies muffle *Gridiron? Bloody Hell.* Gridiron = American football. Americans over-enunciating and barking at each other.

Such over the top expression of two countries I have allegiance to. Being here, right now, makes me feel…lonely.

So lonely.

I watch the cricket. Some of the matches last five days. This adds to my sadness. I have no idea why.

And what is the Pavlovian response to loneliness? Heading toward the bar.

But I see Craigo.

I start winding through the crowd toward him. To my friend. He will make me feel better.

We've only been apart for thirty minutes, yet I have so many questions. *Craigo, why does cricket take a week to play? Craigo, you know I don't watch football; why did you pick this bar? Craigo, are you as happy to see me as I am to see you?*

But he is not.

"Hey! Do you want a Coopers or…"

He takes one more step toward me.

Cocks back.

Swings.

Lights out.

•

I wake up to being in a headlock.

I don't know what he's doing, but I know that I need to follow.

I need to wake up. To fully wake up.

But what do I want? To let Craigo choke me out and to fall asleep.

"He shagged my sistah! The bloody twat!"

Now it makes sense.

I struggle, trying to escape his grip, but he's too strong.

"Craigo, I'm sorry! I'm so sorry."

"Fuck the fuck off, bloody sepo!"

Hands grab us. Very, very strong hands.

And then more hands. Big guys. They are enjoying it. We get pulled apart. I am not resisting whatsoever, but some guy makes a big show. My eye has swollen completely shut.

•

"Didjya want tah press charges? I'd advise against it, since you've both clearly been on the piss all day."

Some local beat cops have us separated. I can sense a crowd. Now, my bad eye is seeping over into the good one.

"No, no. We just got too drunk. I'm as much at fault…"

I say some stuff, and it sounds convincing. I hear a younger cop, who thinks he's out of earshot, gossip with some onlookers: *The Yank shagged his sistah. Lit 'em up like a bloody Christmas tree.*

"Yah mate says he'd like to shake hands. Sluff it off to 'boys will be boys.' You a'right with that?"

"Absolutely. He's my ride home."

This makes the cop smile, and he gives me the briefest glimpse of sympathy. But it's very brief.

Because I fucking recognize him. A fishing and sex tourism buddy of Philip Morris's.

I'm terrified of getting caught, but I want to take a swing at him.

I'm also baffled at how composed he's being. The result? I'm paralyzed.

"You should have that eye looked at. It's gonna be real shinah."

"Yeeeah." I'm stymied at this high-functioning, almost charismatic, pedophile.

I need to get out of here, before I do something stupid.

He looks me over once more and nods. He's playing his role. Professional.

The energy in the crowd has defused, but it's not gone. It's hard to win anybody over, when you're the guy that slept with the other guy's sister. Nobody takes that guy's side. And now I know why Craigo picked Ravesis. So there wouldn't be a five hundred Aussies on one Yank riot. *Didjya hear the sepo was rooting the guy's sistah? Bloody wank.* Here, with the NFL fanatics, at least a quarter of the guys would be responding: *Dude, I dunno? She sounds kinda hot!*

A pretty fucking bulletproof alibi.

Well played, Craigo.

•

"You. Two. Bloody. Idiots."

Suzanne does not look thrilled to be picking us up. Nice of the other cop to call her. Although, I think he and the rest of the force wanted to see the woman that launched a thousand ships.

"Suzie, couldjya pop by Kemeny's on the way? Fresh out of Coopahs at home, and I'm thirsty. You want anything Georgie? You look parched." Craigo is chipper, like he just finished church and is on his way to a wet brunch.

"Yeah, I uh…kinda thiirr…"

"You two? Shut the fuck up." Seeing Suzanne irritated is amusing. Seeing myself in her rearview mirror reaffirms that I don't need to do any explaining. At least not tonight.

She navigates the few short blocks to Craigo's house.

"Look at Georgie's face!"

"He's a bit worse fah wear, ay?"

"Get out, you dickhead."

"Thanks fah the ride, love! And a bit of ice, ay Georgie?" He turns to give me a smile, but stops halfway, looking at my eye and chafed neck.

Being in a chokehold becomes the first commonality I share with Philip Morris.

## 14

The goddamn birds.

I'd forgotten how hard it is to sleep late in my own room.

I overplayed my drunkenness last night. And that killed Suzanne's motherly instinct to baby me. She went to bed and closed her door. I sipped one last beer in the quiet house, letting the condensation of the back-to-back bags of ice drip down my shirt. It took the swelling down.

But it didn't do a damn thing for the bruising.

"Mornin' Gosso."

"Georgie! Ooof. Yah eye. Lovah's quarrel? Did she take a swing atcha, the cheeky black widow?"

He's already making my drink.

"Thanks for the sympathy?"

"Seriously, what happened?"

"You should've seen it last night. Got it surfing, yesterday. But the funny thing is, I'm still hooked."

"Oh, nice one! Yah first time?" He knows I'm lying, but he gives it to me.

"No, but it was the first time I really caught a wave. You know, and rode the actual curl."

"Welcome to the club."

He slides the macchiato over and goes to work on my second.

He drops the teeniest of coy smiles and asks about Suzanne's drink.

"Shall I pop in a piccolo fah takeaway, while I'm at it?"

"Yeah, please, thanks."

And whether or not he heard about what went down last night, he already knows the whole story. At least the town's version of it. Or my face's version of it. He hits the frother with a flourish and beams.

"Aw, mate! I've got a little pressie for yah! Watch the shop for a quick sec?"

"Sure."

He runs to the back. I hear a box being cut open.

He's back with a miniature bring-your-own shopping bag, with a little divider—explicitly made for carrying two coffees.

"Thanks Gosso. It's weird you guys would make such a specific bag, but it's kinda cool. Practical."

"You don't get it?"

"Nope."

"It's fah holding cappuccinos!"

He's so excited, I think he might do a cartwheel.

"Got it."

"Mate, didju wake up to the birds today?" He's dragging it out.

"Yeah, how'd you…"

"And I just gave you a 'cap sack'?" I finally get it, but I let him roar it out. "Is thaaat myyy caaap saaack?"

I join him for the chorus.

"Naaah."

•

Suzanne is pulling the coffee grounds from the cupboard, as I walk in. She welcomes the piccolo, unsure if she's supposed to be mad at me.

"Thank you." She takes a hot sip. "How's the eye? Looks bettah? But ooof, so dark."

"Yeah, I won't be taking any selfies today."

"What happened last night? Yestahday? Didju end up speaking with Philip? Is that why you two idiots ended up on the piss all night?"

I'm glad she's not too mad and even gladder she didn't greet me with a kiss. Because if she was tending to me like a lover, I don't think I could keep it from her.

"No, yeah, yeah. We talked to Philip Morris, who remains a complete asshole. He was fucking livid, but he also didn't want to be outed. So I guess our plan worked?" She nods. None of this is a lie, yet. But I quickly realize that this won't be enough detail for her. She'll keep asking. Unless…"Then we got super fucked up and got into a fist fight about you."

"About me?"

"Honestly, I don't totally remember. But it's cool now. Craigo, he…"

Her eyes pop, defensive.

"What did he say? Why? That meddling little wank! I'm ringing him right now."

"No, Suzanne, wait. I…"

She starts looking for her phone.

Fuck.

If she digs in, we'll bury ourselves in lies. This will never work.

Unless…

Unless she's mad at me.

She finds her phone.

"Suzanne! Shawna is pregnant. That's why he…"

"Whaaat?"

"Shawna. You know how she came out to Panama? I dunno, several weeks ago? She's la…"

"You've got yah girl up the duff at home, and yah're busy keepin' yah manhood warm in me!"

She cocks back. I stay still, positive that she's not going to hit me.

Wrong.

"Fuck! Ow!"

She hits my already destroyed eye and runs upstairs. It hurts. But it also felt good to tell the truth. For once.

Craigo is gonna be pissed.

•

We lead a separate existence for a full day. Sharing a house with a hostile female is brutal, but I hole up and tinker with some work.

---

**From:** Rogers, Timothy

**To:** Lewis, George

**Subject:** Quick touch base

George—

Apologies for the delay, year-end is hectic here in the office. For expediency, allow me to address your questions from several days ago numerically, as well as add my own.

1. Instagram has been abuzz for ages around here. We've dabbled a bit but not been able to crack it. We normally separate photographic content from narrative content. This may sound archaic, but we still do produce a print magazine that hasn't become obsolete, and we can't quite figure out how to merge the two. Your combo journalistic/adventure suggestion might be a possibility. See #2.
2. Regarding the "life skills" suggestions you've made, those are always popular. We have a team that focuses on such immersion journalism, for lack of a better term, where the novice-to-mastery of jujitsu/snowboarding/surfing/building your dream car would sit and where such a piece would be fostered. I'll ask them the next time I have a chance. Even though I'm your boss, getting one of those pieces is pretty dreamy, so I'm all for it, as long as it does not impede you from keeping up with the Tweets.

3. The last I heard, that team was looking for someone to document traveling around the U.S. in a van. But I suspect your nomad lifestyle is waning, and you're ready to have an adult apartment and slightly settle down. Right, Peter Pan? ;)
4. Do let me know if you reconsider NYC for Christmas. It is not to be missed.

Enjoy Rudolph being impersonated by a kangaroo or however they do it down there.

TR

PS Southern Cross—any luck?

---

Never trust anyone who is nice and gives you lots of options. Because they might be sincere. And the options might be real. And then all you have is yourself to blame, when you don't take them.

For now, at least, I'm headed in the right direction. I'm not sure I'm as stable as TR speculates (or hopes), but I do know that I'll be in the *Esquire* offices in January. Collecting my business cards. Signing up for health insurance. And becoming a legitimate human being, who happened to have covered up a murder.

Did he say get paid to drive a van around the U.S.?

---

**From:** Lewis, George

**To:** Rogers, Timothy

**Subject:** Aquatic Southern Cross

Tim—

Thanks for checking in. I will follow your lead and respond numerically (but not respectively) to your list, as it is also my preferred way to categorize thoughts:

1. Indeed, I will be there in January. I will email Lydia after Christmas, when I'm in LA, to sort out any remaining logistics. Her relentless efficiency is inspirational. If there's some sort of group Christmas gift for her, I'd love to contribute.
2. Thank you, again, for the offer to spend Christmas in New York. It's more tempting than you realize. But I need to go home and sort out a few things on the family front. Next time.
3. Any of those life skills assignments sound amazing. And although my wanderlust is quenched for the moment, you should never tease a rolling stone with a paid van trip. Not to worry, I've got the Tweets down and really enjoy the work.
4. Re: #3 Instagram would be a great channel for the van immersion journalism piece. Even if it's not me writing it, that'd be the perfect digital media vehicle to follow an analog vehicle down the road. Sorry for the cheesy metaphor.
5. Still on the theme of life skills, I did learn to surf on this trip. And later the same night, after I caught my first legitimate wave, I went for a dip and saw the Southern Cross. There's something magical about celestial maritime navigation. Thanks for suggesting I keep my eye out for it, as I don't know that I'll be back in Sydney

anytime soon.

Catch you in the New Year.

Best,

George

PS I'm picturing you and your lovely lady attending many fancy NYC Christmas parties and being the toast of the town.

---

Isn't corporate George so nice?

It felt good to tell him about seeing the Southern Cross. And my poor man's surf lesson from Craigo. Even though it wasn't date-specific, it still felt like a slight betrayal of Craigo. Of our secret. But it also felt good. Like letting a few bubbles out underwater, when you take too deep of a breath and can't let it all out.

Not only has TR been abnormally quiet, so has Shawna. It does make me wonder if maybe she wants this baby. Or maybe she wants an abortion. But the one thing I know for sure is that she absolutely doesn't want to do either alone.

Her not responding to my flight itinerary is odd.

---

**From:** Georgeous

**To:** Shawna B.

**Subject:** you can have anything you want

from the airport gift shop for christmas. because even if i could find you something here, i'd not be able to fit it in my bag. amazon gift card?

your mom will be receiving whatever wine i can afford in duty free. i have seen her drink champagne from a can (it's so handy that they come with straws). i'm hoping she won't judge.

i've now seen pj's daughter charlotte a few times. it's surreal. i'll have to tell you about it in person. she is gorgeous. and there's something charming about PJ having a legacy.

all for now.
see you soon.
your george

---

I click *Send.*

Then I reread it.

Giving her the teeniest glimpse of my time here is something. I should have done a better job at it, while I was here. But getting sweet on PJ's sister, Craigo and I killing a guy and mentally severing the last remnants of our relationship (without telling her) were all grenades. Still, I picked the wrong thing. I mentioned Charlotte. I forgot that she might have her own little Charlotte zygote in her belly. Insensitivity is the most regretful, when it's unintentional.

And the sign off with: *your george*? It was honest and second nature but maybe not the ideal salutation, given the scenario.

Let me illustrate my lack of foresight:

*"Charlotte! That is such a cute name. Don't you think it is a cute name? For a girl? If she's a tomboy, you could call her Chuck!"*

*"Totally. We can pick up a baby name book if you want. As long as it's what we read in the waiting room of Planned Parenthood. Wait, you know how they say 'No earrings, No pregnant women' on the rollercoaster rides at Magic Mountain? Maybe that'd be way cheaper? Just remember not to wear earrings that day."*

*"YOU. ARE. SUCH. A. FUCKING. ASSHOLE."*

Pretty accurate, right?

Maybe it's why my job, at times, is so easy.

*@inamedmycatmandu why are women so curious? they have to know everything! does it ever end? it drives me insane.*

*@AskEsquire A woman wanting to understand you is not a crime. Tired of answering? Try asking her a few questions about herself.*

•

"George? You there?"

"Arrgh…yeah…yeah…just dozed off."

"It's fah you. Craigo."

She hands me her phone and walks back to her room. It's incredible how vast the chasm between us has become. Even the smallest thing, like Suzanne calling me George versus Georgie—it stings. And it's only been a day. It's funny, as my black eye dissipates, I'm reminded more of hurting her feelings than taking two headshots from Craigo. Or murdering a guy.

"Hello?"

"Georgie. How you going?" But he isn't really asking. Just habit. He interrupts himself. "Hey, when you were with Suzanne, at Vee's place? You did send those snaps to yahself, right?"

"Yeah?"

"All of 'em?"

"Yeah? Just one sec, lemme check."

I check my Gmail.

"Yeah, they're all here. Want me to forward them to you or…"

"Nooo. Just leave'em. Vee said Philip hadn't returned from the fishing trip. Was a bit worried. Called me."

His all-business calm does the opposite of comforting me. My mind spirals. Will the lack of the shower curtain raise a red flag? Who knows what other evidence we left behind.

"And?"

"I told her what happened. Bit of a chat. Took off. Got on the piss."

We're both too paranoid to say anything over the phone that could be construed as expressing involvement or guilt. Again, Craigo and I would make a great team.

"I wanted to tell her about the photos, but I didn't want to over-worry her. Holding off fah now. Just checking in, in case anyone asks."

I suspect Craigo is fearful of the repercussions of Philip Morris's colleagues. The other dudes in those photos. Also with young girls. And if they're cops, and Craigo ends up speaking to the cops, he needs to know that they can't erase the evidence. That it'll find some sort of higher punitive power. Internal Affairs or whatever they have here in Australia. Internal Affaiyahs.

"Yep. Cool. Did you say anything to Suzanne?"

"Didju?"

"Just what happened. That Philip Morris was pissed but that he didn't want to be outed. I didn't get into what we should do next."

I'm still being ultra-cautious on the phone, but even hearing Craigo's breathing, I can sense that he gets it.

"We're good fah now, mate. Told her mahself that the man-twat would be gone past the holidays. And that I'd figure out the next step with our attorney aftah New Year's."

"OK. Good. Good. Thanks for doing that."

We just killed a guy and hid the body. No biggie. And my biggest concern is hurting the woman whose heart I've already broken. Hurt her more, that is.

"Hey, didju already pack up? You leave on Chrissy mornin', right?"

"Yep. I started packing and then gave up and took a nap. You gave me too much swag from the shop to fit in my bag."

"Classic. Well pull out that PJ trophy, ay? The one I gave you at the wake? I've got somethin' else that's bettah."

"Sure, yeah. I could use the room."

"Georgie?"

"Yeah?"

"You told Suzie, eh? About the kid?"

"Yeah. Sorry. I…I…just…it just came out. And she is pissed. Super pissed. But I'm glad I was honest."

"That was bloody stupid. You couldn't wait? Not a week? Two weeks?"

"You're right. I can't explain why, but I had to tell her. To give her something. I'm sorry."

Silence. But not the bad kind.

"She'll be right. She'll recovah. Maybe just a little TLC before you leave, ay?"

"Yeah, totally. I was gonna go talk to her this afternoon."

Lie.

"That's a good mate."

"Craigo, I'm sorry. Seriously."

"Yah're sorted. All good. I'll pop by tomorrow. Sorry I'll miss you on Christmas morn'. Gotta pull out all the stops fah Hannah."

"Totally. No worries."

"The life of a single dad. You'll be in the same boat soon, Georgie!"

"Fucker."

"Awww. Have a real go."

"Take care, Craigo."

He hangs up.

Suzanne's iPhone returns to the main screen. She's got seven unread texts. I'd say I'm tempted to look, but I'm not. I'm curious. But I don't want to see them. I don't want to know.

I lock her phone, so I can't change my mind.

I shuffle toward her room. Time to erase the lie I told Craigo and make it a truth. The five minute version of the five second rule. Like the lie I told him fell on the ground and I picked it up in time.

But I drag my feet. Delaying it. It makes me feel weak. A man without purpose. A foot shuffler. And there's only one thing worse than a foot shuffler: a nostril flarer.

I look down at her phone. Her screen is cracked. It reminds me of a busted windshield—it only takes a pebble to crack it. But once cracked, it grows. It grows until it spans your entire line of vision, and it needs to be replaced. It distorts your vision. But you can drive a long time with it cracked until it finally shatters.

Confessing to Suzanne about Shawna was me throwing the pebble.

"Hey, thanks for your phone."

She's getting ready in her bathroom, with its unlimited collection of potions and creams. Her bathroom is the front part of her room, which makes me conclude that she was either listening to me or listening for when I finished. Both of which I had already suspected. Just as Craigo feared the wiretap, my wiretap stands in front of me looking irritated, curious and very attractive.

"Sure thing."

"Suzanne, I'm sorry. I'm so sorry." She lets me continue. "I didn't come here with the intention of starting something with you. But we did." All of a sudden, I'm so thirsty, I want to lean down and drink out of the tap, but that won't go over so well. I muscle through it. "And once I was here, I realized that I wanted to escape Shawna. I don't mean from a distance; I mean for good. Did I succeed? Absolutely not. But my failure in relationship management is now second to the situation she's in. I'm not even sure that she is pregnant. She's just late.

And scared. And I have to respect that, because I was part of it."

She softens, slightly. But I know I have to keep going. Not to win her back, just to have her back. To be present. To validate whatever we had.

"She was sick and taking some super specific antibiotic that diminishes the effectiveness of the pill. It was only six weeks ago, but it feels like forever. I swear I didn't come here even remotely thinking…" She snaps.

"Is she an idiot? Does she not read the side effects before popping a pill in her mouth?"

"I know. I felt the same way. No, I mean…I'm not gonna disparage her. I'm still part of it. I just…I just wanted to say that I'm sorry. I've enjoyed my time here. And my time with you." Her face balks, so I improve it. "Plus, I think you're wonderful."

"George. You hurt my feelings. I can't remembah the last time a bloke made me a coffee or a cup a tea. All they evah want is a late night shag. I nevah thought I was gonna move to the States to be yah bride. I just wanted to believe in men. And you gave me hope. It broke my fairytale a bit. You know?"

"I do. And I'm so, so sorry."

"Sorry 'bout the eye?"

"Are you?"

"Nah, not really, love."

She breaks with a smile.

I stare at her, a little sad myself. We got into a rhythm so quickly. And it'll be gone in twenty hours. It's tempting to postulate the future.

*What if? Hey, someday…do you think you'll ever come to the U.S.?*

But it'll only do damage.

And I've done enough.

Oddly, I keep forgetting about Philip Morris. And when I remember him, all I can think of is: 1. please god let us not get caught, and 2. I'm so glad that fucking prick is off the planet. Zero remorse.

"If I try to give you a hug, are you gonna hit me?"

# 15

After a chaste midday spoon session with Suzanne, I know that I have to get up and do some errands. Laying around with her is addicting. But it's also dangerous. I anticipate her asking about Philip Morris. I'm not wrong.

"Georgie?"

"Yeah?"

"Craigo mentioned that Philip would be gone until aftah the New Year. Is that what you heard, too?"

"Yep. The gist, anyway."

I wouldn't think that most people would accept this at face value. But Suzanne has the confidence of someone who only asks questions once. I doubt that I will ever replicate such grace in my lifetime.

"So, if we talk to the attorney, about something more punitive, would you be willing to join a conference call, from the States? Might help a bit if…"

"Oh, Suzanne, of course. I'd do anything."

"I know, love. Just checking. It is a bit unnerving."

"It is. But we have a lot of evidence. He won't go unpunished. And at least Charlotte and Vee are in a better position than they were a few days ago."

"Very, very true. I just wish we could do something more drastic."

"I know. Being patient is the hardest with stuff like this. But it's all we can do." My lies of omission are turning into full blown lies.

She gives an understanding nod and half-smile. She saves me from further burying myself, by slinking off to the bathroom.

It's a timely conversation and a timely break. Before she brought up Philip Morris, I started to worry about us. Her and I. That if I kept lounging with her, I might become so intoxicated by her every gesture that I'd try to have sex with her. And that's not a good idea.

Plus I think she'd turn me down.

Or worse, she wouldn't.

"Hey, I'm gonna walk over the hill to Bondi. Pick up a few things for the plane. Maybe have a quick swim at Icebergs."

"Sounds nice. Wanna have a little Chrissy tea at the restaurant there?" I still find it hard to relate to people calling dinner "tea". *Have you had yah tea?* It's so weird.

"Yeah, but won't it be busy? Christmas Eve? I'd rather go somewhere more low-key. Up the hill. In Bronte."

"Panama House?"

"Perfect. I'll meet you there around seven."

"Enjoy yah swim, love."

•

I'm at a complete loss for what to get for Christmas gifts, but I want to leave something. And I can't show up empty-handed for Shawna, even though I've already prepped her that I would. Under-promise, over-deliver.

Walking up Murray Street toward Bondi Road, I catch Gosso clearing some tables and dropping his movie star smile on a couple finishing breakfast. He's still wearing the Santa hat. It's become restaurant-worker filthy, but he could still be the face of a Movado ad.

"Georgie. Twice in one day! Off fah a trek?" He points to my backpack.

It's too easy.

"Is thaaat my baaackpaaack?" And he joins me.

"Naaah."

"It's sooo good, mate! Happy Christmas!"

"Merry Christmas, Gosso."

It seems pointless to tell him I'm leaving tomorrow. I smile and don't break stride.

•

Icebergs has a little sandwich café with a big view. A croissant, soda water and enough room to write my five Christmas cards to accompany the gifts. I wasn't the first person to think of doing some last minute shopping, and they're not my dream gifts, but I'm pleased nonetheless. Mostly because I get to swim at this majestic place one last time.

*Craigo—*

*Just as a star gridiron footballer needs cleats to navigate the field, so does a talented surfer need these for when the sand is too hot. If these aren't your size, feel free to exchange them for a print or something. Please come see me in the States.*

*Your brother,*

*Georgie*

Gift—Aquabumps Havianna flip-flops with Bondi beach scene. I got a pair for myself, too. I have so much more to say to Craigo. But he's not one for sentiment. And, hopefully, it's all stuff he already knows.

*Mom—*

*This photo is my favorite swimming hole in Sydney. Wish you were here to see it.*

*Merry Christmas.*

*Love,*

*George*

Gift—Aquabumps framed photograph of the pool I'm sitting above. My mom has everything, and all I can really give her is a piece of myself. Plus, I'll find this in the garage in six months and stick it in my house. Wherever that will be. Two gifts in one store. Victory.

*Shawna—*

*Probably tasteless but possibly funny? A gift wrapped with love and laughter.*

*g*

Gift—A sale rack maternity t-shirt. It's got a line drawing of a La-Z-Boy and the caption: *It all started with a chair.* A reference to Shawna's favorite movie: *Juno*. It's super fucked up. But it's thoughtful. And it also shows that I know that she is strongly considering keeping the baby. Ooof.

*Charlotte—*
*My name is George, and I am a good friend of your Auntie Suzanne and Uncle Craig's.*

*I was lucky enough to hold you a few times as a baby. You had the wonderful, kind demeanor of your mom and the ocean-blue eyes of your dad.*

*Your dad and I were very close. More, maybe, than I ever realized. There is an American country song from the '90s by Randy Travis called Heroes and Friends. He sings about those two being the only important types of people in our lives. Your dad, for me, was both. It breaks my heart that you will never know him, but I'm also thrilled that you live on in him. He was brave and goofy and had a heart the size of the moon.*

*I can't wait to see you again. Know that you always have a spot to land, if you ever visit the States.*
*With love,*
*George Lewis*

Gift #1: The Giving Tree by Shel Silverstein.
Gift #2: 529 College Savings Plan at Schwab, courtesy of *Esquire*. It's only $50 a month, but it will be worth $10-20k, when Charlotte is ready for college.

It was tempting to sign off as Uncle George, but that's not a title I can give myself.

*Suzanne—*
*You are really hard to shop for. Especially since you, as an artist, can either create what you want or see everything with a sharp, critical eye. Nothing seemed to fit. So please accept this simple token.*

*When I was little, my grandfather used to babysit me after school. He was a tinkerer and always building things. He wore workman's shirts, even on holidays, and forever kept a Parker Pen in the little pen slot. Before marking anything, he'd pull the pen out and click it three times. An odd quirk but I loved it. Even when I was in the other room, watching cartoons, I'd hear him clicking, and it made me feel safe. Cozy. Loved. In our short time together, you have given me these same sensations. The next time you grab the nearest Post-it pad to sketch, give it three clicks and know how much you are appreciated by others and how much of an impact you have, in your own quiet way.*
*Your Georgie*

Gift—Parker Pen from the drug store. Cost: $14 Australian. I carefully removed it from the packaging, so I could use it to write these cards.

I pack it all up, poke at the croissant remnants with my finger and head toward the locker room to get my swim gear on.

•

It's cold, but it feels good. And the sun is cleansing. Preferable to faux-navigating by the stars at night, covered in blood, hoping not to attract a shark, searching for the shore and a glimmer of Craigo.

I get bored in the middle of a set and dive down to the bottom of the pool. It's an unconventional thing to do, especially sharing the pool with other lap swimmers. But the pool is quiet, as it's Christmas Eve, and I can play.

Exhaling and sinking to the bottom, I wonder how Philip Morris's carcass is holding up. My heart rate speeds up. Coming up for air, I look up at Bondi Road, scanning for a police car. Knowing that it's not there. But wondering when we'll know. Fully know that we're off the hook.

Craigo thought changing my flight might look odd.

Stick with the plan.

So I did. Sticking with the plan, generally, would make a great New Year's resolution. For anyone.

•

There's a time in every trip when you're ready to go home. Sometimes it happens on the first day. Usually in the middle. But the best is when it happens the day before you leave. So you can savor it. And really enjoy the motion in between.

I'm ready to go home.

•

Walking up to Suzanne at the Panama House, she's ready for

another glass.

"Hi!"

"Hey! I see you're already on the Chardonnay."

A flirty waitress leaves her with a giggle, after topping up her glass.

"It's Chrissy! I ordered you an IPA."

"Perfect, thanks."

I set my backpack down and pull out her and Charlotte's gifts.

"You look nice."

"Jeans. Flip-flops. And a shirt that is not a t-shirt? I actually have to agree with you. It's the nicest thing I have."

My beer comes.

"Cheers!"

We both take a few sips.

"Mind if I order another one? Thirsty."

"'Course. But be quick about it. She looks a bit like she's debating a threesome with a couple in a booth out the back."

"I saw. Her libido is fierce. She was licking her chops at you, when I walked in."

"Well love, clearly her taste is…" I cut her off.

"Superb." I cheers her and reach into my backpack. "Hey, would you mind giving this to Charlotte? The book for sure. The note may be a few Christmases away."

"I love love love Shel Silverstein."

"Me too." I hand her the boxed up pen. "For you. It's really just a card. It's nothing."

"Aw, Georgie. Craigo and I got you something, too."

"No, you guys shouldn't have."

"It's just a little something fah the plane. Not to worry." She looks a little excited, and a little buzzed. "Shall I open it?"

"Whatever you want. It's no big…" She slices a manicured nail through the envelope. Even the way she tears open the card is elegant. But it begs for a paper cut.

She reads it. And she reads it again. She gets teary, strokes my chest and gives me a big hug.

"There'll be a big hole when you leave, love. A big hole."

•

Suzanne and I drink the awkwardness away for two hours and walk down the hill arm-in-arm. My eyes drift to the random Christmas lights, and I listen to the sound of my flip-flops on a warm holiday night.

Craigo is rifling through the garage for Hannah's gifts.

"Hey guys! Good night?"

"Yeah, it was nice. I love Latin fusion for Christmas dinner."

"Craigo," Suzanne points. "I put them ovah there. Hannah was building a fort in here. I thought she might find them."

"Ah, that's a good girl. Thanks Suzieeeannne." He corrects himself, showing his appreciation.

He turns to me.

"That little runt. If I didn't keep her gifts here, she'd sort them out the moment I tucked them away."

"Uhhh, can you really call a six year old a runt?"

"If she's yah own daughter you can."

"I'm gonna make some tea. You two?"

"Coopahs."

I nod.

He finds the gifts and starts packing them in a big garbage bag.

Suzanne returns and drops the beers. It's the last time I'm gonna see Craigo. She exits gracefully, without ceremony, applying flawless female intuition.

"So, any word? I've been thinking about it all day."

"Shhh. Yeah, so I talked to Vee again."

"What's up?"

"I checked back in with her. I subtly mentioned the stuff we found on the computah. She was upset but not surprised. They sent some of his mates ovah tah Garie tah look fah him, but nothing. Sometime today or tomorrow, he'll be officially missing. She said she might have one of the blokes give me a buzz. Ask me again about our rendezvous."

"Are you cool?"

"Yeah, should be a'right. It's been a few days. That's a long time down there. Lots of hungry beasts."

"Yeah, yeah. I was thinking the same thing. Hey, do you have a portable hard drive?"

"Yeah?"

"Do you know how to replicate his hard drive?"

"Good idea. We should be sorted with the ones in yah email, but we can't be too careful. Wanna at least be able to go up the food chain, in case one of his coppah mates is implicated."

"There might be other stuff on there that I didn't even find. Creepy website bookmarks. More hidden files."

"Bloody creepah."

"Nostril flarer."

"Ay?"

"Nothing."

"Let me pop these in the boot. You got that trophy?"

"Oh, yeah. Lemme go grab it. And stick this under the tree, too?"

"Georgiiie." The Aquabumps flip-flops aren't wrapped, and the box they're in is a dead giveaway.

I avoid the awkward exchange and run upstairs.

Laying across my bed is an enormous surfboard bag. I unzip it, and an old school single fin rests inside, double wrapped in WGB beach towels. The fin is wrapped in one of PJ's t-shirts: Stop sign, caption (underneath *STOP*): *Hoarding all the swagger.*

I grab the trophy, still in the scotch box, and head down.

"Craigo, what the?"

But he puts up a finger; he's on the phone. With a serious face I've never seen before.

"Yeah, yeah. We did. George and I."

…

"My brothah's mate. Came out for the funeral."

…

"Thank you."

…

"To be candid, we thought he'd laid hands on Vee. Seen some

bruising. She didn't admit to it, but a quick scan of his computah came up with some pretty incriminating photos."

…

"Listen, mate. This is my niece we're talking about. I have a right to inquire into her welfare. Make sure the house she's living in is safe."

…

"Undahstood. But I'm guessing you'd do the same thing."

…

Craigo laughs. The guy must've cracked. Maybe he's not one of Philip's rapist buddies.

…

"So what happened? He hasn't shown?"

I'm so fucking impressed with Craigo right now, I can't stand it.

…

"Aw, he was on the piss a'right. A dozen deep, at least, when we got there. A bit of a chat. But he told me to get fucked."

…

"Dunno. Not long. It's a hike out there, though. He's a big guy, with a tempah. Didn't want to push it."

…

"Yeah, yeah."

…

"To be honest, a rough one. Came back for a few and got a bit sideways with Georgie."

…

He turns to me for a second and nods. The story of us drunken fools got around.

"Nah, nah. We're sorted. He's actually right here. Headin' to the States tomorrow, if you wanna…"

…

"Whaaat?"

…

"Suicidal? Nah. Well, I dunno. He was a bit volatile…"

…

"Jesus Christ."

…

"Well, if there's anything I can do."

…

"Yeah, 'course. He'd wanna help…"

…

"Lewis. George Lewis. We're literally having a Chrissy toast with a couplah Coopahs right now, if you wanna speak with him?"

…

Craigo looks at me again and shrugs.

"Works fah a magazine. Esquire. Writes their Tweets. Bit of a romance column."

…

"Ha, no, not a poof."

…

"Yeah, 'course. No problem."

…

"Cheers, mate. Enjoy yah holiday."

. . .

He hangs up. I see his hands and know they're still a little sore. Just like mine.

"Couldn't get 'em to speak with you to save mah life."

"And I am glad. What'd he say?"

"Guess yah mate Philip had a few complaints. Angah management. Bit of a cowboy on the job."

"Shocker."

"Depahtment knew he was a pisshead, but aren't we all."

We cheers our beers. And right on cue, Suzanne comes out with two more.

"Suzanne, holy fuck. Philip is AWOL."

"Ay?"

"Guess the night Georgie and I popped in, he went on a bendah. No sign of him fah a few days. And they found a small fishing skiff a few kilometers from Garie. Smashed up against the rocks."

"Oh, no! Didju speak with Vee?"

"Yeah, Veronica rang me yestahday. She knew we'd scared him off a bit. But I guess his mates said he hadn't even checked in fah work."

"Are they looking fah him?"

"They had to wait for him to be 'officially' missing, to start the police search. Probably why the coppah called just now. But Vee said his mates have already been out lookin' fah him."

"Did he seem a bit, I dunno, reckless when you guys left?" She turns to me to answer.

"Yeah. Honestly, I'm still processing it. But no, he was not elated to be the recipient of a drive-by pedophile intervention, at his vacation home."

"Hmm. It's odd. But I can't say I'll miss any sleep ovah that wank having a bit of angst and worry. He needs to be behind bars."

Craigo and I nod. Hoping she drops it. She does, sort of. She blows on her tea and thinks quietly.

Craigo and I pick up our fresh beers.

"Craigo, I can't take that board. It's too much. I couldn't get it home, anyway."

"Shush. My fathah gave me that board, and I taught PJ to surf on it. It's got a few dings, but it's solid balsa. It'll brave the trip. Suzanne, can you get Georgie a full sized cab or something tomorrow?"

"'Course."

"No need. I can just get an Uber. Don't even need a phone—it works on the computer, too."

"Sorry we can't take you. Hannah will be chompin' at the bit. And we're gonna swing by little Charlotte's first Chrissy."

"No, no worries. Thanks for the board. It's absurd, but I'll take it. PJ was always roasting me about learning to surf. Now there's no excuse."

He tips his beer toward me.

Suzanne looks like she is trying to go back in the house, to leave us with our bro time, but she's enjoying our little makeshift family.

"The guy on the phone asked about me? Esquire?"

"Yeah, just wanted to know how to get ahold of you. In case they had any questions. Yah phone is off, right? Suspended?"

"It is, but I'll turn it back on the minute I land. I'll email you the number, and they can always email me or contact Esquire."

"He wasn't too interested. Just dotting the i's."

"Why would he want Georgie's numbah?" Suzanne raises an eyebrow.

"Because we were the last ones to see Philip."

We pause, chewing on it.

"Well this Kris Kringle has gotta run. Wrap some pressies. Georgie, you'll be missed. You'll always have a spot here in Sydney."

"The same for you. Seriously, Craigo. Thanks for everything. The board is ridiculous. Gorgeous."

"Aw mate, with all of yah work at the shop, think of it as payment at a dollah an hour."

We hug, but briefly. The Aussie way. Craigo turns to Suzanne.

"See you tomorrow, love."

He gives Suzanne a kiss on the cheek—the tenderest I've ever seen him with her.

Craigo grabs the patio gate and turns to me.

"Georgie, tight lines."

I looked it up. *Tight lines* is a fishing term. You get a tight line from having a fish on the hook.

"You too, Craigo, you too."

# 16

I pack. Sip another beer. Spend a sleepless hour in bed.

I fall into that sleep where you dream you are trying to get yourself to fall asleep. Anxiety dreams are worse than being awake.

A whisper.

"Georgie."

Suzanne. Wearing full pajamas. Like a grandpa might wear, but these are silk and fit her. Every single thing she does is so damn cute.

"Hey."

"Asleep?"

"Not really."

"Wanna spoon?" I open my mouth to say something. I have no idea what. She saves me. "Just come. It's yah last night."

"OK. Yeah. That sounds nice."

We walk down the hall, crawl into bed and intertwine ourselves like a tangled rope. The closeness…it feels incredible.

I wake at 4am. Suzanne is grinding her ass into me.

She turns toward me. I think she's going to kiss me, but she skips it. She removes my clothes and her bottoms with speed and grace. Her top stays on.

And then she fucks me.

Not for me, for her.

She writhes on me, using my dick and hips like a cat scratch tower, bending my penis, cutting off its blood flow and then bringing it back.

It's like she's trying to break me.

Or break up with me.

And then she comes.

She drops off of me. I hear her panting. I wonder if she's even awake. I'm close, but I have to just wait it out.

In three minutes, she's asleep.

And I am not.

I walk down to my bathroom.

Lying down on the floor, I take five strokes and I'm back—fully erect. Fifteen more and I'm done. I'm glad I did it before the plane ride. You don't want to spend fourteen hours needing to release the hostages and to consider doing it, while an air marshal waits outside the bathroom door.

4:30am.

I rinse off, because I'm bored.

I don't bother trying to go back to sleep. Being tired on that long ass flight will be a good thing, anyway.

I fire up the computer, a little spacey. Leaving has me feeling weird and reflective. A good time to give love advice.

*@dayquil_addict what's the broadest advice you could give us? for all situations? so we don't forget? like even just five words?*

*@AskEsquire Listen more than you speak.*

I leave that in the queue for a reread in a few days. I open my emails. Shawna has resurfaced.

---

**From:** Shawna B.
**To:** Georgeous
**Subject:** Bambino? BambiNO

Hey—
It is so odd that you will read this on Christmas, and that is still a day and a half away here.
Anyway, I feel super weird, but I had to tell you, I'm not pregnant. I got a monster period today. Like twice a normal one. I don't know if the pregnancy naturally terminated or what. Literally one hour before my doctor's appointment.
I feel sick and fucked up and, I don't know, relieved?
But I'm sure you will feel relieved, even if you lie to my face and say you aren't (which I would not judge and would actually appreciate).
Regardless, better to know now. You must be flying soon.

Sorry for the ramble.

It's gonna be a weird Christmas.

No matter what, I'm looking forward to seeing you.

I love you.

Your Shawna

---

My shoulders drop, like I just took off a backpack full of rocks. I was not excited about becoming a dad. But there is definitely a sense of loss.

Something.

I don't know.

What's even more haunting is her signature: *Your Shawna.* It's the same way I signed Suzanne's card. I grit my teeth at the guilt. Then I remember; it's also the same way I signed off with Shawna, in my last email.

Well played, Georgie.

•

"Georgie! Get up! Get in here!"

"Huh?"

"Get in here!"

After playing on the computer, I ended up crashing in my own bed and even slept through the goddamn birds. I walk toward Suzanne's room, and I can hear the news on TV.

Suzanne is transfixed.

Philip Morris's cadet photo is onscreen, a side shot next to the anchor woman. The caption: *Decorated Officer Found Dead at Sea.*

"Philip LeCompte's body was found by divers early this morning. Although his body has suffered damage from feeding marine life, investigators have suggested the cause of death as a suicide or possible accidental overdose…"

"Holy fucking shit."

This is the best morning of my life.

"Isn't it awful?"

Nope.

"Yeah, sad, I guess?"

"Earlier they said the fishies had a field day with him, not much there…disgusting."

And once again, the water is my friend.

"Wow, that's brutal. Do you want some coffee?"

"The guy is dead! Isn't it weird that you guys went there to…"

I cut her off.

"I know. But he was a jerk. And a fucking rapist. I'm sorry if I don't get all sympathetic. I didn't like him when he was here. Neither did you, Suzanne."

"Yeeeaaah." She pauses for a moment. Then she looks back at the TV. Then at me. "Sooo, what time didju guys leave? Garie?"

"Uh, it was, uh, like dusk-ish? It was dark, but…"

She looks me in the eyes.

Fuck.

She reaches for my forearm, tenderly. She drags her fingers down the bullet scar on the back of my hand. From Panama. From PJ. She lingers, almost sensually, on my wrist. I keep my hand closed, in a fist.

Although they're barely visible, I don't want her asking about the earphone cord marks on my palm. For a moment, it feels like we are about to have goodbye sex, but she's just putting the pieces together. And touching me is telling me she's giving me the benefit of the doubt.

"Suzanne. The thing is…"

She kisses me, shutting me up. She pulls away. And locks eyes with me.

"Georgie, whatevah happened, it doesn't mattah. No one's holding a vigil ovah that wank." She kisses me on the forehead. "We've got time before yah flight. Why dontchya make yahself useful? Go make us a coffee."

•

Coffee cups on bedside tables, we wake from our morning nap. A nap with a little extra.

I make two fresh cups and walk back into Suzanne's room.

I can hear her in the shower. I set her coffee on the edge of the sink counter, attempting to give her privacy.

"I made more coffee. Setting it here."

"Ah! You scared me."

I pop my head around.

"One full frontal. Please?"

"Georgie, you pervert!" But her irritation is exaggerated. "A'right, make it quick."

"So beautiful."

I walk up and give her a big wet kiss, getting my t-shirt soaked.

She giggles.

"Yah're gonna miss yah flight!"

"I know. I'm gonna go shower."

•

Toweling off in my room, there's a wrapped box on my bed.

*Georgie—*

*You will be missed.*

*Happy Christmas*

*Craigo & Suzanne*

I open it. Bose Noise Cancelling headphones. For the plane. Wireless.

•

Suzanne is late. Her phone buzzes with texts from Craigo to *Hurry the fuck up!*

I knew the moment I read Shawna's note that I wouldn't tell Suzanne. There was no point. Other than to torment her. Maybe in a month. With a nice email.

We say goodbye at the door to her little car. No promises. No future plans. Just a long hug. A sweet kiss. We say goodbye like adults.

"Travel safe, love."

"Will do. Merry Christmas, Suzanne."

She drives away. And I wonder if I'm walking away from one of the great loves of my life. I catch a glimpse of her eyes in the rearview. I don't know if I'm looking for a tear, but she's already put her sunglasses on. I wonder if she caught the one rolling down my cheek, before I wiped it away.

•

The Uber driver is gracious with the huge surfboard; he's done it many times before. He doesn't even comment about the nose of it resting against his shoulder, as he drives.

"Nice holiday?"

"Yeah, it was. Magic. I'm sad to leave."

"Well you can always come back, mate! First time to Sydney?"

•

I've got my backpack, a roller bag and the massive surfboard, as I enter the linoleum of SYD. My heaviest baggage? Knowing that I'm an accessory to murder. An accessory I'll wear forever. And it itches.

A few surfer bros nod, like I came to shag some Aussie chicks and grab some waves. I smile. But it's forced. Because they're right. At least on paper. But it couldn't be less true. Not for me, it's not.

Airports take me one of two ways, emotionally. Either to the excitement of the trip ahead or the sadness of being in between. Right now, I feel the latter. I remember in fourth grade when my grandfather died. The same one who clicked his pen three times at every task. When he passed, I got called out of class and had to walk home. Even as a little boy whose mom still cut his hair, I knew. I knew I had lost my best friend.

Walking home that day, I prepped myself to interact with a lot of people. And I knew that people would be sweet. I knew that I could eat anything I wanted, even cookies for dinner. With my little head down, I didn't care. Even at that young age, I recognized that most of life was made up of moments like this. Moments when you're transient. You're always heading somewhere, toward others. Toward companionship. That these moments are brief. But they make up the true weight of life, and you spend them alone.

I look at the departures board. My flight is on time. My ticket, thanks to *Esquire*, is fully exchangeable. I look back at the board. There's a flight to New York in an hour. I could just make it. I could take TR up on his offer.

I think about it for a second, then shift my backpack, shift the surfboard. I see my own reflection. The fading shadow of my black eye.

Not now.

Now it's time to go home.

• • •

# Acknowledgments

I spent almost two months in Bronte. Its stunning beauty is only matched by the warmth of its inhabitants.

My editor, Jennifer Lewis, is as helpful as she has a penchant for giving her opinion in all caps. May you never *OMIT!* me from our friendship.

Pilar Alessandra, my writing coach, teaches me how to keep things more true to Georgie and slightly less Jason Bourne.

Maddy Hutchison is a ray of sunshine and a comma hawk.

Toby Petersen, clinical snarkiologist, is as forthcoming with crisp design as he is with the quips.

Ushma Domadia is an expert in character development and puppy fanaticism.

Gergie, Jenn & Jessie Miller were tremendous with their hospitality, during my accidental extended stay.

Craig(o) Wright was gracious enough to let me butcher his good name and is adept at descending invisible stairs.

David Henstock offered to pay for my Obamacare during the long rounds of edits and is perpetually an inspiration in critical thinking and creativity.

Glenn Allen makes my problems disappear, including installing televisions and cleaning carpets.

Thank you for your open doors and inspiration: Aquabumps, Beach Road Hotel, Beats by Dre, Berocca, Bondi and Bronte Swim & Lifesaving Clubs (SLSC), Bose Corporation, Coopers Ale, Cooper's

Market & Café, Esquire Magazine, Favoloso Café, Gertrude & Alice's, James P. Carse, Icebergs, Kemeny's, Mini Moke, Molte Cose, The Panama House, Parker Pens, Ravesis and Victoria Bitter.

# About the Author

Thomas with Bruiser at Muttville, San Francisco. Photo by Julie Stiefel.

Made in the USA
Middletown, DE
11 June 2024

55612383R10156